D1381416

LEGION
LIES OF THE BEHOLDER

Also by Brandon Sanderson from Gollancz:

LEGION
LIES OF THE BEHOLDER

BRANDON SANDERSON

GOLLANCZ

LONDON

This edition first published in Great Britain in 2018 by Gollancz.

First published in Great Britain in 2016 by Gollancz
an imprint of the Orion Publishing Group Ltd
Carmelite House, 50 Victoria Embankment
London EC4Y 0DZ

An Hachette UK Company

1 3 5 7 9 10 8 6 4 2

A CIP catalogue record for this book is
available from the British Library.

ISBN hardback 978 1 473 22496 4
ISBN eBook 978 1 473 22497 1

Printed in Great Britain by Clays Ltd, Elcograf S.p.A.

www.brandonsanderson.com
www.gollancz.co.uk

LEGION
LIES OF THE BEHOLDER

ONE

"So . . ." J.C. said, hands on hips as he regarded the building. "Anyone else worried that this doctor's office is in a slum?"

"It's *not* a slum," Ivy said, extending her hand to help me from the back of the limo.

"Sure," J.C. said. "And those *aren't* crack dealers on the corner over there."

"J.C., those kids are like *six*."

He narrowed his eyes. "Starting early, are they? Nefarious little entrepreneurs."

Ivy rolled her eyes, but Tobias—an African American man who was growing a little unsteady on his feet, now that he was getting on in years—just laughed a hearty, full-throated laugh. He climbed out of the limo with my help, then slapped J.C. on the back. They'd been joking the whole way here.

J.C. grinned, showing he was at least a little aware of his buffoonery.

I eyed the building. Though it was your typical, generic suburban office structure, it *was* across the street from a pawnshop and next door to an auto mechanic. Not a slum, but hardly prime real estate either. So maybe J.C. had a point.

I rapped on the front passenger window of the limo, which rolled down, revealing a young woman with short blonde hair. Wilson's grandniece was shadowing him again. Right. I wished he'd left her behind today; I tend to be a little more . . . erratic when visiting with reporters.

I looked past her toward the tall, distinguished man in the driver's seat. "Why don't you wait here, Wilson," I said, "instead of going to the service station? In case we've got the wrong location or something."

"Very well, Master Leeds," Wilson said.

His grandniece nodded eagerly. As comfortable as Wilson looked in his traditional buttling gear, she seemed awkward wrapped in a coachman's coat and cap. Like she was playing dress-up. Had she been listening as I talked to my hallucinations in the back seat? I was used to Wilson, but it felt wrong to expose myself to someone from the outside. I mean, I was used to people seeing my . . . eccentricities when I was in public. But this felt different. An intrusion.

I turned and walked with my aspects into the office building, which had a familiar, sterile quality. Not quite like a hospital, but scrubbed often enough to give it the off-white scent of one. The first door to the right was number sixteen, where we were supposed to meet the interviewer.

J.C. glanced in through the side window. "No reception area," he said. "Just one large room. Feels like the sort of place where someone grabs you the moment you walk in. You black out, and then . . . BAM . . . three kidneys."

"*Three?*" Ivy asked.

"Sure," J.C. replied. "They need unwitting mules for their illegal organ trade."

"And exactly *how* unwitting are you going to be when you wake up with an incision in your abdomen? Wouldn't you immediately run to the doctor?"

His eyes narrowed. "Well, the doctor's obviously *in on it*, Ivy."

I looked to Tobias, who was still smiling. He nodded toward a painting on the hallway wall. "That's by Albert Bierstadt," he said. "*Among the Sierra Nevada Mountains.* The original hangs in the Smithsonian, as one of the most famous works of the Hudson River School." His calming tone was a relaxing contrast to J.C.'s jovial—but still deep-seated—paranoia. "I've always loved how the clouds part to illuminate the dark wilderness: a representation of the Creation through the lens of the American frontier. Our eyes are inexorably drawn toward that central light, as if we are being accepted into heaven."

"Or," Ivy observed, "perhaps the clouds are closing, and the landscape is dimming as God withdraws and leaves men in darkness."

Startled, I glanced sharply at Ivy. She was usually the religious one, sticking up for all things Christian and holy. She shrugged and looked away.

I knocked, and the door opened to reveal a tall, mature Asian woman with a square face and prominent smile lines. "Ah! Mr. Leeds. Excellent." She gestured for us to enter, and J.C.—of course—went first.

He ducked under her arm, deftly avoiding touching a real person, then looked around, hand on his weapon. Finally he nodded for the rest of us to enter.

The interviewer had set out a group of chairs for us, and she stood by the door a conspicuously long time for all of us to enter. She'd done her homework. Though she waited too long—she couldn't see the aspects—her effort did help with the illusion, for which I was grateful.

Ivy and Tobias settled themselves while J.C. continued to inspect the room. Large windows to our right looked out on the curb, where Wilson stood beside my limo. The far left wall of the room was dominated by a large saltwater fish tank. The rest of the décor was in a "writing den" theme, with hardwood bookcases and deep green carpeting.

I stepped up to the window and nodded toward Wilson, who waved back.

"Three today, then?" the interviewer asked.

I turned around, frowning.

"I followed your eyes," she said, pointing to the chairs where Ivy and Tobias sat, then to where J.C. had been standing—though he'd moved to search the bookshelves for secret passages.

"Only three," I said.

"Ivy, Tobias, J.C.?"

"You *have* done your homework."

"I like to be prepared," the woman said, settling down in her own seat. "I'm Jenny, by the way, in case Liza didn't say."

This woman was Jenny Zhang, reporter and bestselling writer. She specialized in salacious pop-biographies that rode the lines between information, entertainment, and voyeurism. She had won awards, but really, she was just another hack who had fought her way out of the clickbait trenches and earned a measure of respectability.

I wished I'd never promised Liza the favor of doing an interview with one of her friends, but I was stuck. Hopefully Jenny wouldn't keep me too long, and her eventual book wouldn't be *too* painful.

She nodded toward the seats, but I remained beside the window. "Suit yourself," she said, getting out a notepad. She pointed at my aspects. "J.C., Tobias, Ivy. Id, ego, superego."

"Oh, *great*," Ivy said. "One of those. Tell her we've been over this. It doesn't fit."

"We're not fans," I said to Jenny, "of that psychological profile."

"Ivy's the one complaining?" Jenny asked. "She's a repository of your understanding of human nature—you've externalized in her your people skills and your understanding of relationships. She's reportedly very cynical. What does that say about you, I wonder?"

I shifted uncomfortably.

"Hey," J.C. said. "That's not bad."

"But you've also created a personification of peace and relaxation." Jenny pointed her pencil toward one of the seats. She had them reversed, but obviously she meant Tobias this time. "You say he's a historian, but how often does his knowledge of history prove relevant?"

"Frequently," I said.

"That's not what I hear," Jenny said. "You claim to have limited 'slots' in a given team of aspects. Imagining too many at once is difficult, so you bring only a few with you at a time. Yet you always take these three. J.C.—your sense of paranoia and self-preservation—is a logical inclusion. As is Ivy, who can help you cope with the social norms of the outside world. But why Tobias?"

"She knows too much," Ivy said. "Something's wrong with this interview."

"Do we really need to panic?" Tobias said. "So she's read the previous profiles people have done of Stephen. Surely, we should expect that. Wouldn't we be more suspicious if she hadn't come in with some theories about our nature?"

I idled by the window, but finally J.C. nodded and sat down. He was satisfied. I stepped away from the window, but didn't sit. Instead, I walked up to the fish tank. It was extravagant, with variegated corals and beautiful lighting. So much work to create what amounted to a prison.

Jenny was writing on her notepad. What *did* she find so fascinating? I'd barely said anything.

I watched the fish pick at the coral, eating at their own confines. "Don't you have any other questions for me?" I finally asked Jenny. "Everyone else wants to know how I distinguish reality from hallucination. Or they want to know what it feels like to assimilate knowledge—then manifest it as an aspect."

"What happened to Ignacio?" Jenny asked.

I spun on her. Tobias raised a hand to his lips, gasping softly.

"You mentioned Ignacio in past interviews," Jenny said, watching me with poised pencil. "One of your favorite aspects. A chemist? And yet, in your recent case with the motor-oil-eating bacteria, you didn't involve him at all. Curious."

Ignacio. He, like Justin, was . . . was no longer one of my aspects.

Tobias cleared his throat. "Did you see she has an Algernon Blackwood book on the shelf? Original Arkham House edition, which is my favorite. The feel of the paper—the scent . . . it is the scent of lore itself."

"You've frozen up," Jenny noted. "Can you *lose* aspects, Mr. Leeds?"

"Original Arkham House editions are . . . are rare . . . though that depends on who you want to read. I once had a copy of Bradbury's *Dark Carnival* from them, though the cover . . ."

"What happened?" Jenny asked. "Did they simply move out?"

"The cover . . . did not . . . age . . . well. . . ."

"Ivy," I whispered.

"Right, right," she said, standing up. "Okay, so she's acting like this is an innocent question, but I don't buy it. She knew this would touch a nerve. Look how tightly she holds that pencil, hanging on your words."

"I'm sorry," Tobias said, dabbing at his brow with a handkerchief. "I am not helpful right now, am I?"

"She's goading us," J.C. said, standing up. He rested his hand on Ivy's shoulder. "What do we do?"

"She wants to push us off balance," Ivy decided. "Steve, you need to reassert control of the conversation."

"But *how much does she know?*" Tobias asked. "Did she really guess what happened to Ignacio? You don't speak of these things often." He cocked his head. "Stan says . . . Stan says she must be working for *them*."

"Not helping, Tobias!" Ivy said, glaring at him.

"Quiet," I said to them. "Quiet, *all of you*."

They quieted. I locked eyes with Jenny, who now sat calmly twirling her pencil between two fingers. Feigned nonchalance.

I couldn't keep unraveling every time Ignacio or Justin came up. I had to control this.

I was *not* crazy.

"I'm not comfortable talking about this topic," I said, finally walking over and taking the seat she'd provided for me.

"Why not?"

"Different question, please."

"Have you lost any aspects besides Ignacio?"

"I can sit here all day, Jenny," I said. "Repeating the same words over and over. Is that how you want to waste your interview?"

The pencil stopped twirling. "Very well. Another question then." She shuffled through her papers. "You've maintained throughout all your interviews that you are not insane—that by your definition, 'insanity' is the line beyond which an individual's psychology impinges upon their ability to live a normal life. A line you've never crossed."

"Exactly," I said. "The media pretends that 'insanity' is this magical state that is simply on or off. Like it's a disease you can catch. They miss the nuance. The human brain's structure and chemistry are incredibly complex, and certain traits which—in the extreme—are deemed insane by society can be present in many so-called normal people, and contribute greatly to their success."

"So you deny that mental illness is, indeed, an illness?"

"I didn't say that." I glanced at my aspects. Ivy, who sat down, primly crossing her legs. Tobias, who stood and strolled over to the window, looking up to where he thought he could see Stan the astronaut up in his satellite. J.C., who had moved to lounge by the door, hand on his gun.

"I'm just saying," I continued, "that the definition of the word 'insanity' is a moving target, and depends greatly upon the person being discussed. If someone's means of thinking is different from your own, but those thought patterns don't disrupt their life, why try to 'fix' them? I don't need to be fixed. If I did, my life would be out of control."

"That's a false dichotomy," Jenny said. "You could be both in need of help *and* in control."

"I'm fine."

"And your aspects don't disrupt your life?"

"Depends on how annoying J.C. is being at the moment."

"Hey!" J.C. said. "I don't deserve that."

All three of us looked at him.

". . . today," he added. "I've been good."

Ivy cocked an eyebrow. "On the way here, you said—and I quote—'The police shouldn't be so racist to them towel-heads, because it isn't their fault they were born in China or wherever.'"

"See, being good." J.C. paused. "Should I have called them 'towel-headed Americans' or something . . . ?"

"Your id is speaking out?" Jenny looked from me to J.C. She was good at following my attention.

"He is *not* my id," I said. "Don't try to pretend he somehow articulates my secret desires."

"I'm not certain he can *articulate* anything," Ivy added. "As doing so would, by definition, require more than grunts."

J.C. rolled his eyes.

I stood up and walked over to the fish tank again. I always wondered . . . did the fish know they were in a cage? Could they comprehend what had happened to them, that their entire world was artificial?

"So," Jenny said. "Perhaps we could track your status, Mr. Leeds. Three years ago, during your last interview, you said you were feeling better than you ever had. Is that still the case? Have you gotten better, or worse, over the years?"

"It doesn't work that way," I said, watching a little black and red fish dart behind some fake yellow coral. "I don't get 'better' or 'worse' because I'm not sick. I simply am who I am."

"And you never before considered your . . . state . . . to be an affliction?" Jenny asked. "Because very early reports paint a different picture. They describe a frightened man who claimed he was surrounded by demons, each whispering instructions to him."

"I . . ."

That had been a long time ago. *Find a purpose,* Sandra had taught me. *Do something with the voices. Make them serve you.*

"Hey," J.C. interrupted, "I'm gonna go grab some jerky or something at that gas station. Anyone want anything?"

"Wait!" I said, spinning away from the fish tank. "I might need you."

"What?" J.C. said, hand on the doorknob. "Need me to be the butt of more jokes? I'm sure you'll live."

He stepped out, then pulled the door closed. I stood, speechless. *He'd actually left.* Usually when J.C. disobeyed, it was because I tried to leave him behind—or because I didn't want him practicing with his guns. He disobeyed to protect me. He didn't just . . . just walk away.

Ivy ran to the door and peeked after him. "Want me to go after him?"

"No," I whispered.

"So," Jenny said. "We were talking about you getting worse?"

I . . . I . . .

"That's an Achilles tang," Tobias said, stepping up to me and nodding toward the little red and black fish. "It looks black, but it's actually dark brown, sometimes even a dark purple. A beautiful, but difficult fish to keep; that spot on the tail is the origin of its name—as it looks a little like a bleeding wound on the heel."

I took a deep breath. J.C. was just being J.C. We were talking too much about aspects—and he hated being reminded he wasn't real. That was why he'd left.

"I've had some rough patches lately, perhaps," I said to Jenny. "I need something to focus my aspects and my mind."

"A case?" Jenny said, pulling a few sheets out from behind her notepad. "I might be able to help with that." She set the sheets on the coffee table in front of her.

"Ah . . ." Ivy said, walking over to me. "That's her angle, Steve. This is all preamble. She wants to *hire* you."

"She was pushing you off balance," Tobias said with a nod. "Perhaps to get herself into a better bargaining position?"

This was familiar ground. I relaxed, then walked over and settled down in the seat across from Jenny. "All this to offer me a case? You people. You realize that you can just *ask*."

"You have a tendency to return letters unopened, Leeds," the reporter said, but she did have the decency to blush.

"What is this . . ." I said, skimming. "Machine that can use big data to predict a person's exact wants, updated minute by minute, incorporating brain chemistry with historic decisions, removing the need for most choices . . ."

"Kind of interesting," Ivy said, reading over my shoulder. "I guess it will depend on what she's willing to pay, and what exactly she wants us to do."

"What do you need from me?" I asked Jenny.

"I need you to steal a—"

My pocket buzzed. I absently glanced at the phone, expecting a text from J.C. He'd probably sent me a picture of himself trying to drink straight from the soda machine at the gas station, or some similar nonsense.

But the text wasn't from J.C. It was from Sandra. The woman who originally taught me to use my aspects; the woman who had brought me sanity. The woman who had vanished soon after.

The text read, simply, *HELP.*

TWO

I tore from the room, followed by Ivy and Tobias. Out on the street, Wilson and his niece saw something was up, and he alertly opened the car door for me. I waved Ivy and Tobias in. J.C.? Where was J.C.?

No time. I climbed into the back seat of the limo.

"Wait!" Jenny shouted from the door of the building. "What about my interview! I was promised a full session!"

"I'll start it up again another time!"

"But the case!" she said, holding up her papers. "I need to see how your aspects respond to this situation. Aren't you intrigued by—"

I slammed the door shut. On a normal day, perhaps I *would* have been intrigued. Not today. I held up the phone for Ivy and Tobias.

"You're sure it's from her?" Ivy asked.

"It's from the number she left on the table that morning," I said. "I've kept it in my contacts list on every phone I've had since." We'd tried tracing it in the past, but phone records always listed it as un-assigned.

Wilson climbed into the passenger-side front door, and his grand-niece pulled on her coachman's cap and took the driver's seat. The car rumbled to life. "Where to, sir?" she asked.

I looked from Tobias to Ivy.

"It could be someone else spoofing the number," Ivy said. "Be careful."

Is it really you? I typed to her.

Destiny Place, she typed back. It was her nickname for Cramrid Hotel, the place where we'd first met. Another text soon followed: a sequence of numbers and nonsense characters.

What? I typed to her.

No reply.

"Sir?" Wilson asked from the front. "We're leaving?"

"Take us home," I said to Wilson.

His niece pulled us out onto the street and made a U-turn, heading back the way we'd come.

"What are those numbers?" Ivy asked, looking toward Tobias. "Do you recognize them?"

He shook his head.

"Sandra is worried that I might not be the one who has the phone," I said. "It's a cipher. She often did this sort of thing."

The other two shared a look. Both of them had been around when I'd known Sandra—or at least they'd been among the many shadows and apparitions I'd seen back then. But they hadn't been *completely* themselves until Sandra taught me to create aspects. Focusing my attention, meditating, compartmentalizing my mind. They'd transformed naturally from shadows and whispered voices into distinct individuals.

"We should ignore it," Ivy said. "She's playing with you again, Steve. If that's really her."

"If he ignores it, Ivy," Tobias said softly, "it will haunt him for the rest of his life. You know he needs to pursue this."

Ivy sat back, folding her arms. With her blonde hair in a tight bun and her no-nonsense pantsuit, you might easily think her cold. But when she looked away out the window, there were tears in the corners of her eyes.

Tobias placed his hand on her shoulder.

Oddly, I felt out of place. I should have offered her comfort, reassured her I wasn't looking for a cure, or a way to be rid of her. I'd always promised Ivy that wasn't the point of finding Sandra.

I did none of this. Instead, I stared at the phone screen. *HELP.* Twelve years ago, Sandra had saved me from the nightmare my life had become. Dared I hope that I'd be able to be with her again? Dared I hope that she'd be able to do something about the way I was sliding, my aspects getting worse, my—

The image on my screen was obscured as a new text popped up.

Dude. DUDE! Tell me I didn't just see you drive off.

We're heading home, I wrote to J.C. *Grab an Uber or something.*

I got you a doughnut and everything. With sprinkles.

And you haven't eaten it yet?

Sure I did, he wrote back. *But I knew I probably would, so I bought two. Can't promise the second will survive the trip home. These are dangerous times, Skinny, and it's a rough neighborhood for a tasty doughnut to be wandering about on its own.*

J.C., Sandra just texted me. She needs help.

I didn't get a response for a good minute and a half.

Stay at home until I get there, he wrote.

I'll try.

Skinny. I'm telling you, wait.

I tucked the phone into my pocket. Three more texts came from him, but I ignored them. I wanted J.C. to hurry, and nothing would make that happen more efficiently than letting him think I was going into danger without him.

Not that there was anything he'd be able to do. He was a hallucination, not a real bodyguard. Though . . . there *had* been that one time, when he'd moved my hand—as if he were controlling it. And that time he'd pushed me out of the car . . .

I texted Kalyani en route, so the aspects were waiting by the windows when I got back to the mansion. I pushed open the car door as soon as we were near the house. Wilson's niece yelped, then stopped the car.

I strode across the lawn.

"Want me to get the White Room ready?" Ivy asked, hurrying up.

"We don't have time for that," I said. "Get me Audrey, Ngozi, Armando, and Chin."

"Got it."

We reached the front doors, and I took a deep breath, bracing myself. All of my aspects would be here. That could—*would*—be taxing.

"Master Leeds?" Wilson asked, stepping up to my side. "Might I discuss something with you?"

"Can it wait?" I said, then pushed open the doors.

It hit me like a sudden weight—as if someone had slipped bars of lead in my pockets. Some fifty people, standing inside, all talking at once. Some were panicked. Others excited. A few haunted. The same name was on all their lips. Sandra.

Tobias joined me, and he seemed winded. From that short walk from the car? He *was* getting old. What . . . what happened when one of my aspects died of old age?

"Can you quiet the crowd?" I asked him.

"Certainly," Tobias said. He stepped among them and began

explaining. His calming voice worked for most of them, though as I walked up the stairs of the grand entry hall, one woman broke off from the others and chased after me.

"Hey," Audrey said. Plump with dark hair, she tended to be a little unusual even for an aspect. "Sandra's back, eh? Is she going to un-crazy you? I'd like forewarning if I'm going to vanish forever; I've got plans for tonight."

"Date?" I asked.

"Binge-watching *Gilmore Girls* and eating like seventeen bowls of imaginary popcorn. I can't *technically* gain weight, right, since I already weigh nothing?"

I smiled wanly as we reached the top steps.

"So . . ." she said. "You doing okay?"

"No," I said. "Take this, see if you can figure out what this sequence of numbers means." I tossed her the phone.

Which, of course, she fumbled and dropped. I winced. Audrey looked at me sheepishly, but it wasn't her fault. My mind had *forced* her to fumble it—because she wasn't actually real. I'd thrown my phone toward empty space. It had been a while since I'd made that kind of mistake.

I picked up the phone—its screen had cracked, but not badly—and showed Audrey what Sandra had sent. Audrey was the closest thing we had to a cryptographer. Actually, she was getting pretty good at it, now that I'd read a few more books on the subject.

"Thoughts?" I asked.

"Give me a few minutes," she said. "Those characters in the string are probably wildcards . . . but for what . . ." She scribbled the string on her hand with a pen. "You going to deal with that mess?" she asked, gesturing toward the aspects down below.

"No," I said.

"You going to at least count who didn't show up?"

I hesitated, then leaned against the banister and did a quick count, already feeling a headache coming on. No Armando, but that wasn't odd. He rarely left his room, or his "kingdom in exile" as he put it. Ngozi had come, which was good. She wore a face mask and gloves, but Kalyani had been working with her—and they'd been going out lately. Like, the actual outdoors.

Let's see . . . no Arnaud, he's probably sitting in his room, oblivious as always. No Leroy. Isn't he on a skiing vacation? No Lua. Maybe in the yard, working on his hearth? He'd been constructing his own "stone age" house in the back yard, using only technology he could build by himself.

I hastened through the second floor's hallways to Arnaud's room. The light above the door was on, indicating that he didn't want to be disturbed, so I knocked. Finally he answered, a diminutive balding man with a soft French accent.

"Oh!" he said. "Monsieur!"

"How's the device, Arnaud?" I asked.

"Come and see!" He opened the door, letting me into his laboratory. There were blackout curtains over the windows, since he was frequently developing film these days. Bits and pieces of machinery were neatly laid out on the workbench. A cigar in an ashtray indicated that Ivans had been helping him. He was the only aspect that still smoked.

Taped to the wall was a series of pictures. Winter scenes of the mansion.

"I've only been able to get it to go back about six months at most," Arnaud said, stepping over to a device sitting on the table: a big old-school camera, like the ones you'd see news photographers use in old movies. "Just as you surmised, the flash is the most important part. But I still haven't figured out exactly how it penetrates time."

I took the camera, feeling its weight in my hands. A camera that could take photos of the past. The device had been involved in one of my most dangerous cases.

"I've now fitted it with instant film," Arnaud said. "It should work. This dial here? That sets the time focus. It's most accurate at short range, just a few days. The farther back you go, the blurrier the pictures become. I do not know how the original inventor solved this, but so far, I am at a loss. It is perhaps related to moments blurring together the farther back we try to make the light penetrate."

"It'll do, Arnaud. It's fantastic." I glanced to the side and noticed a few prints on the ground, each cut in half. "What are those?"

"Oh." Arnaud shuffled, looking embarrassed. "I thought it would be good to have Armando look them over, as he is the expert in photography. I know physics, but not the taking of good shots. Armando agreed and destroyed several of my photos, as they were not 'significant' enough."

I sighed, then packed the camera in a bag that Arnaud pointed out. Part of me already knew that the device would be ready. I'd been spending evenings in this room, working with my hands as Arnaud instructed me on the repairs. But those sliced photos were new.

I was getting very, *very* tired of Armando's shtick. Each of my aspects could be challenging in their own way, but none were so outright disobedient.

I shouldered the camera. "You did well, Arnaud. Thank you."

"Thank you! I am pleased to hear it." He hesitated beside the door as I opened it. "Could I . . . return to France now? And my family."

I froze. "Return?"

"Yes, Étienne. I understand how important our work here was, and it was truly engaging. But my job, it is finished, correct? I could return now?"

"You want to . . . leave. Not be an aspect any longer?"

"If it would not be too much trouble."

"I . . ." I'd never had an aspect want to leave, other than for a brief vacation. "Let me get back to you. I mean, I won't keep you here against your will, but the camera isn't completely finished yet. Maybe . . . maybe we could work out . . . for your family to come here . . . or for you to live part-time back in Nice?"

"Thank you," he said.

I pulled the door shut, troubled. Wilson walked up, bearing a tray of much-needed lemonade. "Master Leeds," he said. "I *do* need to talk to you about a small matter. Insignificant, really, but I don't want you growing too distracted to . . ."

I took a long pull on a glass of lemonade, then slung the camera bag off my shoulder. "Would you pack this camera in the car for me, Wilson? I need to talk to Armando. I'll make time to chat with you then, all right?"

I just . . . Sandra. I had to keep focused on Sandra.

Sandra had *texted* me.

I checked the phone again as I walked up toward Armando's attic room. Nothing more from Sandra, just a few texts from J.C., complaining that his Uber driver had a "Gun-Free Zone" sticker on his car window.

As if that means anything, J.C.'s text said. *You can't simply "sticker" your way out of the Constitution, buddy.*

It was followed by: *And yeah, I just ate your doughnut.*

I shook my head, knocking at the attic door. No response from Armando. Was he imposing "royal auditory sanctions" on me again?

I pushed the door open, preparing myself to be shouted at. Armando claimed to be the rightful emperor of Mexico, and . . .

His room had been destroyed.

And there was blood on the walls.

THREE

Gouges in the plaster, like the claw marks of a feral beast. The bedding had been shredded. Stylish night photographs from cities around the world—Armando's prize collection—lay in confetti on the floor.

And the blood. Sprays were flung across nearly every surface. Suddenly, I felt thoughts fading from my memory. Knowledge and expertise dispersed like smoke from a snuffed candle.

I'd first gained Armando about eight years ago, when working on a missing person case. A woman had vanished, but then continued to upload selfies with famous monuments—though the security footage showed she'd never been at any of them. I'd used Sandra's technique, binge-reading about photo manipulation and imagining the information as a reservoir within me. I hadn't consciously created Armando, no more than I'd consciously given any of the aspects personalities, but he'd been the result. In the early days, we'd joked about his claim to the throne of Mexico, just as I now joked with J.C.

I felt that reservoir leaking away like blood from my veins. I grew cold and stumbled backward, horrified by the scene of carnage inside his room. I couldn't . . . I had to . . .

It was gone.

He was gone. I fell to my knees and let out a low moan that became a cry of agony. A breeze through the room's open window blew scraps of torn photographs into the hallway around me.

Mi Won was the first to arrive. She gasped, but—ever the professional—went inside to assist anyone who might need her medical skills. The other aspects began arriving in a steady stream, gathering around me, though in that moment . . . in that moment they seemed to fade into the background. A group of shadows. Mere silhouettes.

"Master Leeds!" Wilson said, rushing up. He passed right through several of the aspects, then knelt beside me. "Stephen? Please. What is wrong?"

Slowly, I let my hands relax. I let out a long sigh, and felt a strange calm come over me. I had to keep control. That was . . . that was what Sandra taught me.

"Wilson," I said, surprised at how even my voice sounded, "what was it you wanted to talk to me about?"

"Oh, never mind that! Sir? What is wrong? Why did you cry out?" He peered into the room.

"What do you see?" I whispered.

"Sir? It looks like it always does. Empty guest room. The bed made with a yellow comforter, tucked in."

"Pictures on the floor?" I asked.

"No, sir. Would you . . . like me to pretend there are?"

I shook my head.

"Sir, if I may say, you've been *most* strange lately. More, I mean. More than usual." The elderly butler wrung his hands. Behind him, his niece stood in the mouth of the attic stairwell, looking at us uncertainly.

"Am I causing it?" Wilson asked.

"Causing it?" I asked, blinking.

"Because of . . . today, sir."

"Today?"

"My retirement, Master Leeds. We've discussed it. Remember? It was going to be last month, but you asked me to stay on. But sir, today, I'm *seventy* today."

"Nonsense. You can't be . . ."

Retirement? We'd discussed it?

I could vaguely remember . . .

Mi Won left Armando's room and shook her head. The other aspects brightened into full color again, and their worried chattering suddenly filled my ears. Ivy pushed through them, then stepped toward the room. Mi Won grabbed her arm.

"I'm sorry," Mi Won said. "He's gone."

"What kind of gone?" Ivy demanded, then turned toward me. "Justin and Ignacio didn't just *go*. They became something else, something terrible. It's happening again, isn't it, Steve?"

I hauled myself to my feet, using the wall for support. "I can't . . . I can't keep imagining you all right now. Go to your rooms. Everyone who isn't on the mission. Ngozi, Ivy, Tobias."

"Did you want me?" Chin—Chowyun Chin—asked. He was wearing sunglasses as always, no matter the time of day.

"Sandra was always fond of puzzles," I said to him, "and so I might need to crack some computer codes. I want you and Audrey to stay ready and near her phone. But I think . . . I think I can only manage a few of you with me today. Please."

"Sure," Chin said. "You've got those new programs installed?"

I wiggled my phone. We'd been making enhancements.

"You cracked the screen?"

"Sorry."

He sighed, but then—with the others—retreated. Fifty figures, each distinct, each a chunk of my mind. People with lives, pasts, families, passions. At times, it was just *so much* to track. Kalyani gave me a hug as she joined Rahul. Ivans gave me a fist bump. Oliver let me hold his stuffed corgi, which I did for an embarrassingly long time, before they finally left me.

I tried to imagine what this was like for them, discovering that for the first time in years, I was losing control. That Sandra had returned—a figure who to most of them was mere legend.

Wilson looked on, helpless, though his niece—Barb—was more visibly disturbed by it all. Ivy studied her, shaking her head.

He's been training her for months now, I thought, remembering. *Because he's retiring. Leaving me.*

"Wilson," I said. "I . . . I realize—"

I cut off as I spotted something. The withdrawal of most of the aspects left a conspicuous figure standing in the hallway, holding a notepad. She was tall, Asian, and wearing a relaxed pantsuit. Jenny Zhang. The reporter.

I lurched toward her, shoving past Wilson and grabbing her by the shoulders. "How did you get in here!" I shouted, feeling betrayed, embarrassed. How *dare* she see me at my most vulnerable!

"You broke our promise," she snapped. "I need to get this down. For the book."

"Steve?" Ivy said.

"What book?" I said to Jenny. "I didn't give you permission to write a book! You're trespassing!"

"Steve, I think she can *see us*."

I froze, my eyes locked with Jenny's. Then she turned and looked right at Ivy.

"Wilson," I said, growing cold, "can you see the person I'm holding right now?"

"Master Leeds? Is it one of your aspects?"

"*Can you see her?*"

"No. Unless you wish for me to . . . to pretend?"

Oh hell.

"What did we do earlier today?" I said to Wilson. "Where did we go?"

"Sir? Barb and I drove you around a poorer section of town, and we stopped at an abandoned building. I must admit I was worried, though grateful you told me to stay close by. You stood in an empty room for a while, then came running out."

I let go of Jenny, who straightened her jacket with an unperturbed air.

I put my hand to my head. It wasn't possible. I wasn't supposed to be crazy. The aspects . . . shielded me from that. *They* were insane, and I kept them organized. I . . . I could tell what was real. . . .

"Was Sandra real?" I asked Wilson.

"Yes, sir," he said. "You've never questioned that before. . . . Master Leeds? This *is* caused by my leaving, isn't it? I'm sorry. But sir, I just can't keep doing this. Not after the case with that assassin, and then the fire last year. Barb, though, she's *excited* to help you. She'll be good at it, sir."

I stood there until the sound of footsteps announced Tobias's arrival. Ivy ran to him and whispered to him, and the old historian nodded, running a hand through his powder-white hair. Then he smiled.

"It's all right," he said. "He's bound to be a little upset. Why, we've finally found Sandra!"

Ivy whispered something else, and Tobias glanced at Armando's room, lips pursing grimly. Then he smiled again, walked over, and gripped me—gently but firmly—on the shoulder. "Strength, Stephen. Let's pull through this. You can do it. You've always been able to do it."

"Armando . . ." I whispered.

"It happened. We just have to make sure it doesn't happen again. *Focus.* Sandra has returned."

I looked to Ivy, who pointedly did not look at Armando's room. "I think . . . I think maybe I've been wrong. You're right, Steve. We need to find Sandra. Maybe she's back for a reason; maybe someone up above is watching out for us."

Nearby, Jenny was writing all of this down. How on Earth had I created her? And why?

"Wilson?" I asked, showing him my phone. "Yes, I know it's cracked. Not that. The text."

"Help," he read, tilting his glasses and squinting. "And a sequence of numbers and letters. From . . . Sandra?"

I sighed in relief. So the text was real. Unless . . . unless Wilson was a hallucination too.

I couldn't go down *that* particular rabbit hole. I had to believe I had at least that shred of sanity left.

"Where's Ngozi?" I asked Ivy.

"Didn't you see her back off? The sight of the blood . . . I think she's getting some air."

My forensic scientist was a germophobe who couldn't stand the sight of blood. My brain was a very strange place sometimes.

"See if you can find her," I said to Ivy. "I want her along. You, her, me, Tobias, J.C.—once he catches up."

Ivy nodded and ran off.

"And me," Jenny noted.

"*Not* you," I said, walking toward the stairwell. Tobias walked with me and kept his hand on my shoulder, as if I were the frail old man, not him. We passed Barb and I looked her up and down. Short blonde hair, perky grin. So young. "I haven't scared you off?" I asked.

"Honestly, this is really interesting," she said. "You are *so* crazy."

"Go start the car and wait for me."

She ran off, and I looked back at Wilson. "Can she at least make lemonade?"

"My own recipe, sir. And I must say, she's taken to it with acumen." He hesitated. "Perhaps I could add another day or two—"

"No. This had to happen eventually, Wilson. You've given more than enough. More than anyone probably should have given." I'd already made sure there was something nice in the bank for him— I'd done that years ago, and for some reason, he'd just kept on with me. Perhaps he was the crazy one.

I started down the steps with Tobias. From above us on the stairs, Wilson watched us go. "Sir," he called after me. "If, for some reason, you aren't fighting terrorists or finding teleporting cats tonight, I would love to have you at the party. My brother is hosting it."

"A party?" I said, looking over my shoulder. "With *real people*?"

"The best kind, sir."

"Yeah. I'll pass. But thanks anyway."

F O U R

I haven't always been this bad about real people. It was only . . . what, a year and a half ago that I'd been going out on dates? All had been unmitigated disasters, but at least I'd tried.

Ivy claimed I unintentionally sabotaged those interactions. She had all kinds of theories as to why, none of them particularly flattering.

I found Audrey, Chin, and a few of the others in the game room. It was a place they could be around each other for mutual support in facing what was coming. Stormy was making drinks. Entering the room, I braced myself and tried to keep my focus. Sandra. Sandra would know how to help me.

To be honest, I'd been sliding for months now. Maybe years. But I *could* turn it around.

Near the bar, Audrey had her feet up on an ottoman, chewing on some Sugar Babies candies while watching cat videos on her phone. Ever since J.C. had gotten a phone, the rest had wanted one—except Harrison, the technophobe.

"Check it out," Audrey said, showing me a cat meowing as its owner opened a can of food—then stopping abruptly every time the owner stopped. "I can't get enough of this stuff."

I just stood there, staring at her.

"What?" she asked.

"We're in the *middle* of a disaster," I whispered. "Aspects are being corrupted, Audrey."

"Yeah. Can't decide if I'll be the next to go, since I know too much, or if it would be more ironic for me to go last."

"You were supposed to be—"

"Relax," she said, showing me a piece of paper. "I cracked it. I needed a key to the cipher, which turned out to be the room number at the hotel where you two first met. With that plugged in, it didn't take long. These are GPS coordinates."

I took the paper with a relieved sigh. "Where is it?"

"City fairgrounds. There's an outdoor performance tonight. Starts in a half hour." Audrey checked her phone. "Right at sundown."

That sounded like Sandra. I tucked the paper in my pocket, then turned to go.

"Hey," Audrey said, "you think . . . maybe you can imagine me a shotgun or something?" She bit her lip. "In case, you know, this goes south? And . . . the nightmares come to . . ."

"That won't happen."

"And if it does?"

"Break into J.C.'s room."

"And set off the inevitable booby traps? You know he has them. Even if we haven't seen them, he has them."

She was right. He probably had a minefield installed under the floor or something.

Audrey chuckled as Stormy brought her a mimosa, and I left, a bitter taste in my mouth. If Audrey was worried, that was very bad.

The halls of the mansion were oddly quiet, contrasting with the disturbance earlier. I didn't pass a soul, human or imaginary, as I walked toward the door. The place felt so hollow, I almost worried that they'd all just . . . vanished on me. Then I heard Ivans shouting from the conservatory, where another group had gathered.

I tried calming myself with some deep breaths, and checked outside. I spotted Ivy and Ngozi near the far hedge. Ivy was very careful not to put her arm around Ngozi, but her posture was encouraging. Eventually, the two walked over.

Ngozi was still wearing a face mask and gloves, but she removed the mask as she stepped up to me. I always forgot how tall she was; she easily had five inches on me. She spoke with a lofty accent, Nigerian with a hint of her British education. "I'm sorry. I . . . panicked."

"Can you handle this?" I asked.

"Yes. If you're sure you need me."

I wasn't sure. I couldn't be sure *what* this case would require—but I had a hunch. Things were never simple when Sandra was involved. And if we couldn't find anything at the coordinates Sandra had sent, Ngozi was our best bet at investigating a possible crime scene.

"I am sure I need you," I said. "But there might be a crowd at the fairgrounds. Are you going to freak out, like last time?"

"Depends. Is someone going to try to give me leprosy this time?"

"*One* person sneezed on you, Ngozi."

"Did you *hear* that sneeze? Do you know how many germs the average uninterrupted sneeze can produce? Projected into the air, hanging like little mines, sticking to your face, your skin, infiltrating your system . . ." She shivered, then held up a gloved hand to interrupt my next complaint. "I can do it, Stephen Leeds. I *will* do it. This is . . . a special case."

Ivy and Ngozi walked to the limo, which was still parked by the curb. Barb was polishing the hood ornament, but she'd left the back door open, in case aspects needed to enter. Tobias sat inside already, reading a thick book to keep his mind off our troubles. That made three. I could handle three.

Four, I thought, checking my phone. There was no response from J.C., so I texted him. *Did you stop to catch a movie or something?*

A response came shortly after. *Stupid Uber stopped and picked someone else up, then drove the wrong direction. I finally managed to get out at Seventeenth and State.*

I sighed. *J.C., did you just climb in a random Uber?*

. . . Maybe.

What were you thinking!

I've got my stealth suit on. They can't see me. Figured I could head the right direction, then get out and take another.

It was as close as he ever came to admitting he wasn't real. Where another aspect would have been fine fudging things a little, catching an imaginary Uber, J.C. . . . well, J.C. didn't play by the same rules. He tried to be real.

Or my brain tried to make him real. Or . . . or I don't know. My head was pounding, and as I composed a reply, a large shadow fell over me. I glanced back and noticed Lua—a three-hundred-pound Pacific Islander—trying to read over my shoulder. Instead of his traditional survivalist gear, he was wearing his Cub Scout shirt. *That's right.* Tonight had been pack meeting. He'd entirely missed the chaos inside.

"Hey, boss," he said. He nudged his chin toward my phone. "You need me? I can do a J.C. impression. Grab a big knife. Glare at everyone."

"No," I said. "Thanks anyway."

"You sure? If we're tracking someone, I can track people."

"We won't be leaving the city—I'm hardly likely to get trapped in the wilderness or something."

"No problem, boss," he said. Then he clapped me on the shoulder. "Hey. Surviving isn't just about making shoes from vines and an oven from mud and stones, you know? Keep your eyes up, boss. Shoulders back."

"I . . . It's getting hard, Lua. Harder every day. My own brain fights against me."

"No. We're your brain, boss. We fight *with* you." Before stepping away, he clasped my arm and then gave me a hug.

And honestly, I felt a little better as I settled into the car. *Meet us at the fairgrounds on Thirtieth*, I told J.C. *That might be easier.*

I suppose, he texted back. *But can't you just wait?*

Just meet us there. Don't take someone else's Uber. Here, I'm sending a cab for you. I had a few drivers around town who were willing to accept large sums to drive to a spot, open the door, then close it and drive an empty car to another spot. I should have done that for J.C. in the first place. I would have, if I'd been thinking straight.

Fine, he sent back. *But be careful. Something feels wrong about all of this.*

I mumbled to Barb where I wanted to go, and she pulled out. But I continued staring at the phone.

"You have to tell J.C. what happened, Stephen," Tobias said from the seat beside me.

But I didn't. Not yet. At least one of us could go on pretending, for a little while, that we hadn't lost Armando. I locked the phone and tucked it into my jacket pocket.

FIVE

Dusk had fallen by the time we reached the fairgrounds, which—this time of year—was just a tramped-down field of dirt on the east side of the city. A large swell of people had gathered as if for a concert—they were common here—but were currently milling among vendors. The performance wasn't to start for another few minutes.

Barb dropped us off at the curb. I absently bought us all tickets—paying for my aspects without thinking—then led us among the evening throng. The crowd made it difficult to see, but announcements were being made from a stage set up on the dirt ahead.

I hated crowds. Always had. It's difficult for my aspects to maintain the illusion when people are milling around, mashed together, breathing the same stale air and conversing in a buzzing cacophony. . . .

So maybe Ngozi came by her germophobia honestly. She stuck closest to me, eyes forward, hand on my shoulder. I was proud of her, all things considered.

Ahead of us, the announcer quieted, and bright flares of light came from the stage.

"Are those *fireworks*?" Ivy asked from just behind us.

"No," Tobias said. He dodged to the side, narrowly avoiding a collision with a little girl who shot past holding an ice cream cone. "I've read about what this is." He gestured to an open spot up ahead.

We took refuge from the crowds under the eaves of a small toolshed for the fairgrounds staff, and I got my first good look at the performance. Men in protective clothing stood on the stage and threw *molten metal* up against a black fireproof backdrop.

The effect was dazzling, and for a moment the crowd seemed to vanish. Even my urgent worry about Sandra faded. The performers would dip a ladle into a bucket of the metal, then fling it up in a burning swirl. When the metal hit the wall, it splashed outward, exploding into thousands upon thousands of glittering sparks. These fell in waves, like molten rain.

It *was* like fireworks, but somehow more primal. No gunpowder or smoke. Just buckets, a steady hand, and perhaps an unhealthy disregard for one's own safety.

"It's called Da Shuhua," Tobias said. "I've always wanted to see the performance in person. The story goes that hundreds of years ago, blacksmiths in Nanchuan, China, had no money for fireworks. So they came up with something else, using what they had on hand."

The performers threw with frantic energy, ladle after ladle—as if they were trying to stay ahead of gravity and get all the fire into the air at once. The explosions of sparks created streaky patterns in the air, like tiny sprites flaring to life for a mayfly existence—one brilliant moment of life and glory, before succumbing to the cold.

"That *can't* be safe," Ngozi said.

"Wonder and irresponsibility are often bedfellows, Ngozi," Tobias responded. I glanced at him, watching sparks reflect in his eyes. "The name Da Shuhua translates to something like 'tree flowers' and implies that you beat the tree and the flowers appear. You take something ordinary and make it *extraordinary*. All it takes is two thousand degrees."

We watched until the performance reached an intermission. The crowd in the immediate vicinity started to disperse, seeking out food vendors or nearby carnival rides. I checked my phone, showing it to the others. Sandra's coordinates indicated a spot ahead near the edge of the fairgrounds.

"We should be careful," Ngozi said. "What would J.C. say?"

"Probably something vaguely racist and/or threatening," Tobias noted.

"No, no, he'd say something like . . ." Ivy adopted a husky voice. "'Guys, stop. Look very carefully. Do you see it? Do you see that? Is that . . . *funnel cake?*'"

Ngozi chuckled. But she was right, we should be careful. Fortunately, I'd prepared for this. I rounded the dusty fairgrounds, eventually positioning us a close—but safe—distance away from the coordinates. Judging by my phone's map, our goal was a small path running near some trampled grass. *That bench*, I thought. I texted Barb, then settled down near some bushes where I could watch the bench without getting too close.

"Ngozi," I said, unpacking some binoculars she could use. "Give that spot a look. Tell me what you see. Pretend it's a crime scene."

"What good is that going to do?" Ivy said. "She can't just *pretend* there's blood around."

"Forensics isn't just used to study homicides," Ngozi said absently, reaching into my pack with her handkerchief, then taking out another pair of binoculars. "The various forensic disciplines are simply studies of the way that science interacts with the law, or applying science to the law." She scanned the area. "I usually start with a question. What about the scene is odd, out of place . . . ?"

I unpacked the camera, then tried to affix it to the tripod—and failed. Damn it.

"That's because you lost Armando?" Jenny asked. "You can't even work a *tripod* now that you no longer have your photo expert?"

I looked up sharply. Yes, there she was, the aspect with the notepad.

"How did you get here?" I demanded.

"Uber."

Sure, *she* could work it out and not get lost. I sighed, then gave up on the tripod. I probably didn't need it anyway.

"How are you going to use that?" Jenny asked, taking notes, narrowing her eyes. "Isn't it the flash that's the important part—the part that lets you take photos of the past? We've set up too far away for that to work."

She was right, but it was also true that I was likely to drop the stupid thing if I tried to take a picture. Losing an aspect left me bizarrely incompetent, particularly right after they left. Eventually, the others could compensate a little.

I'd still never be the same. But again, I'd allowed for that. As Ngozi continued her investigation, I stood up, looking past Jenny—trying to ignore her—toward Barb, who was approaching.

"Wow," she said, chauffeur's cap tucked under her arm. "Did you see those spark things? That was *awesome*."

"I need you to do something that might be dangerous," I said.

"Sure!"

I tried not to let her naive enthusiasm put me off. I should be *glad* she wanted to help, not annoyed. It was just that she felt like the others. Regular people. Who treated what I did as some kind of carnival act.

"There's a bench over there near that hot dog cart. See it?" I handed her the camera. "Leave your cap and jacket here—they're too conspicuous. Go over there and pretend you're taking pictures of the stage and the crowds, but get the bench in every shot."

"Cool," she said.

"Here's the important part," I said, holding up the camera and showing her the dial on the flash that would change the time of day—in the past—that she was taking pictures of. "Rotate this one tick each picture, all right? It's *very important.*"

She rolled her eyes, which didn't inspire confidence, then handed me her coachman's cap and jacket. She wandered off inspecting the camera, which was more user friendly than it looked. Arnaud simply liked a retro aesthetic. Theoretically, the . . . um . . . thing with the . . . er . . . other things . . . wouldn't need . . . to be twisted . . . or . . .

Well, I was reasonably certain it would take pictures just fine for someone who didn't know picture taking.

"Clever," Jenny said. "Using a real person to do what you cannot."

"I am a real person."

"You know what I mean," she said, scribbling some notes in her pad. "Why do you always insist on doing so much alone? If you had a team of real assistants, not just the occasional chauffeur forced to pitch in, how much further could you go?"

Tobias settled down on a boulder to wait, while Ivy demanded that I show her my phone to see where J.C. was—the app tracked the car I'd sent for him. It was at a stoplight nearby, though it appeared to have been caught in the traffic surrounding the festival.

Another round of tree flowers started as Barb was taking her photos. Well, that would just give her some extra cover. Ngozi watched carefully to see if anyone reacted to Barb, and so I took a turn with the real pair of binoculars. Naturally, Ngozi could only notice something if I saw it.

I watched the sparks. They seemed more . . . violent to me this time. Angry. The flashes from Barb's camera and its unique bulb seemed stark to me, flagrant.

I saw no sign of Sandra.

Barb strolled back and delivered the photos, which were starting to develop. "Great," I said, distracted as I looked through them. "Go wait in the car. Keep that camera safe."

"That's it?" she said. "That's all I get to do?"

"Other than wait in the car? Yes."

She took back her cap and coat, and left, muttering to herself. I looked up and found Jenny regarding me, then making another note.

"All right," Ngozi said as I sat down on the boulder by Tobias. "Let's see . . ."

Though it was getting dark, the pictures—all save the first—were during the day. Timestamps at the bottom indicated that each successive picture was a half hour farther back in the past. With eight total, we had four hours of data.

Hopefully Ngozi could make something of them, treating the area as a crime scene. I flipped through the pictures one after another to give Ngozi a glimpse, then we'd spend time analyzing each one for—

That was Sandra.

I froze, holding the next-to-last picture. A narrow face, with almost ghostly features. Her hair was longer and straight, but it was her. Sitting on the bench, reaching toward the wastebasket beside her.

Ivy gasped. Jenny took notes. Ngozi lowered her face mask and pulled off a surgical glove, then rested her fingertips on the picture. Tobias put his hand on my shoulder and squeezed.

She'd been here. She'd actually been here, not four hours ago. But where had she gone?

"She texted you," Ngozi said, "then dropped something in the rubbish bin."

"Then let's go get it!" I said, suddenly heedless of any risk.

"Hold on a moment," Ngozi said, making me check the last photo. "I said *wait*. Tobias, restrain him." She shivered, putting her glove back on as Tobias held me still. His wasn't a strong grip, but there was something demanding about it.

"See here," Ngozi continued. "This man buying a hot dog from the vendor? He's back again in this other picture, and *again* in this picture."

I sat back and squinted at the photos. At a prompt from Ivy, I used my phone for light so we could see them better.

Behind us, the crowd oohed and aahed over another round of sparks in the air.

"So . . ." I said. "He likes hot dogs?"

Ngozi cocked an eyebrow at me.

"Either that," I said, "or both the patron and the vendor are involved."

"Look here," Ngozi said, pointing at another picture. "They're whispering together. They're definitely involved."

My heart sank, and I looked back. The same vendor as in the pictures—a younger black man—was selling hot dogs now. "They're surveying the drop site," I said. "Waiting to grab me, perhaps?"

"Well," Ngozi said, "you're not exactly hard to find. If they wanted to snatch you, they wouldn't do it here, in a crowded area. They'd come to your home, or ambush you on the street."

Ivy grunted. "So maybe they just want to see what you do?"

"Or maybe they're after Sandra," Ngozi said. "Or maybe they don't know who is going to respond to her texts. Or, most likely, they're connected to this in a way we can't guess—because we don't have the right information."

I turned back to the photo of Sandra. Then I stood up and started walking toward the bench.

My aspects scrambled to catch up. "Steve?" Ivy said. "What are you doing? Shouldn't we think about this?"

I didn't want to think about this. I'd had enough of thinking and worrying. Maybe I was making this harder than it needed to be. Or maybe I was doing something willfully stupid, and wanted to be done with it before J.C. got back to stop me.

Either way, I ignored the sputtering aspects as I strode right up to the wastebasket. I dug into it, ignoring the ends of half-eaten hot dog buns—and heard Ngozi retch at my side.

I pulled my arm out holding a small black bag, which turned out to contain a smartphone. It needed a PIN to open—and I tried the room number from Destiny Place, the one Audrey had used in the cipher. It worked, and the phone opened to the photo archive, showing selfies of Sandra sitting on the bench. She'd captioned the last of them.

It's really me. Here is your proof. More to come.

"The vendor at the hot dog cart is right over there," Ivy said from my side. "But I can't find the other man from the pictures. We need J.C. Where *is* he?"

I turned to face the hot dog cart, with its vendor.

"Here we go . . ." Ivy said with a sigh.

"Ngozi," I said softly, "see if you can pick out where this man came from or who he works for."

"It doesn't work that way!" she said. "I'm not Sherlock Holmes."

I ignored her complaint and—as flashes of light behind us lit the fairgrounds a shimmering red-orange—I strode right up to the man at the hot dog cart, placed Sandra's phone on the counter, and looked him right in the eyes.

"I'm tired," I told him. "And I feel old."

The man stood up straight, eyes going wide. He had his hair in a buzz cut, and was lean and muscular. J.C. could have told me whether he was packing, but even I noticed how poor a fit he was for his hot-dog-vendor role.

"Sir," he said, "I'm not certain if a hot dog can help."

Too formal. Military training, perhaps?

I sighed, wiping my hands on one of his napkins. Then I reached for my pocket. He immediately responded by reaching for his gun, flipping back his apron and revealing a holster.

I held my hand back up, splaying my fingers, showing I'd gotten nothing. I nodded toward his gun. "We can stop playing. I told you. I'm too old for this."

"Old?" the man finally said, lowering his hand. "You don't look that old, sir."

"And yet, parts of me are wearing out. Like a car with faulty brakes and a secondhand engine. Looks and runs fine until you put it under stress, and then . . . well, all hell starts to break loose." I spun the phone on the counter, then turned and scared away someone else who got into line wanting a hot dog.

"I think he must be the junior of the two," Ivy guessed, inspecting the hot dog vendor. "See how nervous he is? He was set here to watch and send word if you showed up. I'd guess he wasn't supposed to actually deal with you."

"So who sent you?" I asked him. "And why didn't you just take this phone yourself and run?"

The man shut right up, practically stood at attention, and didn't answer as I pressed further. Yes, military for sure.

"I guess I should go then?" I said, taking the phone.

The man put his hand on it—not pulling it away from me, but also preventing me from walking off with it.

"So you *do* want to talk?" I said. "Then—"

"You can stop bullying him, Mr. Legion," another voice said. I looked to the side as the other man from the photos approached: older, Caucasian, with flecks of grey in his beard. "He can't answer your questions."

"Then who can?" I asked.

The man pointed at the phone. Which started ringing.

I frowned, then answered and held it up to my ear. "Hello?"

"Hey," Sandra said on the other end. "It's good to hear your voice again."

SIX

Sandra.

Sandra.

Her voice was full and husky, like the sound of a solitary cello. It reminded me of peace, of nightmares stilling. Of quiet talks at night, with a candle flickering between us, because modern lights weren't alive enough for Sandra.

"Why?" I said to her. "Why dump this phone here, and go through all of this? Why not just *call me.*"

"We needed a secure line, Rhone."

My middle name. I closed my eyes, imagining lazy days near the end, after I'd silenced and embodied the voices. Days when I got to just lie there, Sandra beside me, speaking softly. She'd always said I wasn't a "Stephen." That was too common a name.

"My line *is* secure," I told her.

"Secure *from* you, I'm afraid."

"So you're working with these men?" I asked, glancing at the two beside the hot dog cart.

"In a way."

"I need to meet with you, Sandra," I said. "I'm . . . I'm not as strong as I was when you left. Things have started to fall apart."

"I know."

"You've been watching me?"

"No. It happened to me too."

"Your aspects. Jimmy, Orca, Mason . . . how are they?"

"Gone."

It felt like she'd punched me in the stomach.

"I need you to go with these men, Rhone," she said. "I need you to trust me. They're working on something that can help you. Has helped me."

The longer she spoke, the more *wrong* she sounded. Like she was drugged or something. I lifted the phone from my ear and pointed for the aspects to gather in closer and listen.

"Sandra?" I said. "What happened to your aspects? What's going on?"

"I gave them away," she said softly. "For sanity. Come see me, Rhone. It's . . . better this way."

I looked up to Ivy, who nodded curtly. I hit mute on the phone, looking toward the two men. The young one was a soldier, but the older one—now that I got a good look at him—didn't have the feel of a security officer. A little too pudgy, a little too relaxed in that sport coat, even if I did spot a gun peeking out from an underarm holster. J.C. would be proud of me.

"What have you done to her?" I demanded.

"Rather," the older man said, "you should ask what she's chosen to do to herself."

"Which is?"

"She's found peace," the man said. "We can offer it to you too. A simple business arrangement. Your brain—safe within your skull, don't look at me like that—and our technology. We can make the world a better place, and your world a saner one, all through the power of our proprietary solution."

"He sounds like a businessman," Tobias said, "giving a pitch to the board of directors."

"He's intrigued by you," Ivy said, eyes narrowing. "Maybe even amused."

I lifted the phone to my ear, unmuting it. "Sandra? I want to talk to you in private. Just you and me. No phones. No listeners."

"And if I ask you for help?"

I felt a sudden need to give back to her. All those years ago, she'd saved my life, and I was desperate to repay our debt. To put us on even footing. Because, deep down, I suspected she'd left because I had been too needy and our relationship had been unbalanced.

She's playing me. She knows how I feel and she's playing me. Help. It was such a *difficult* word to ignore.

I turned away from the two men, speaking more softly into the phone. "Are they holding you? Have they drugged you?"

"If I say yes, will you come?"

"I . . ."

"I almost came back, you know," she said. "Two years ago, when it started going badly for me? I came to visit. But I left before speaking with you. Rhone . . . it's going to get worse for you. You're like me, only a few years behind. The brain, it just can't take the strain. You're going to start losing them again. Unless you submit."

"To what?"

"To a perfect world."

"Well," Ivy noted beside me, "*that's* not ominous."

"Sandra," I said. "It's not supposed to go this way. I've imagined . . . I mean, I pictured . . ."

"Rhone, Rhone . . . You should know by now. The two of us are too good at imagining. But when have the daydreams ever played out as we wanted them to? Go with Kyle."

"But—"

"I'll see you then. Come."

She hung up.

And I realized I was weeping. My arm went limp, and I nearly dropped the phone as I turned toward the two men.

"Mr. Legion," said the older man, who was probably Kyle, "the paradigm you live in *can* be expanded. Please, let me show you the nature of our work, and let it redefine your vision of what is possible."

"You're holding her."

"You'll find that we have done nothing outside the moral and ethical bounds of good business."

I sneered.

"Leeds," Ngozi said, taking me by the arm. Light flared behind us, and the crowd cheered.

"I don't know what you've done to her," I said to Kyle. "But I'm not going with you. I'm going to find Sandra. I'm going to *free* her."

"And if she doesn't want your freedom?"

I snarled. "You can't—"

"Stephen," Tobias said. "Perhaps you should calm down. Deep breaths, remember? Let me tell you a little more about these fire displays. Listen to my voice. The displays are so beautiful because . . ."

I breathed in and out, calming myself to the rhythm of Tobias's words. Kyle and the other man backed off, and I turned to look across the crowd toward the flashes of sparks against the wall. They were beautiful, as Tobias said. I listened to his voice until . . .

What was that chill?

I looked into the crowd. Most everyone was facing the display, but one nearby figure moved in my direction. I frowned as this person walked *right through* a couple—as if they weren't really there. The figure had . . . had sunken eye sockets and pale, milky eyes with no pupils.

His skin had gone ashen white, even faintly translucent, so you could see the shadows of the skull beneath. But I *recognized* that face anyway. Armando.

Armando—what was left of him—howled and leaped toward me, slashing with a large knife. I jumped back, but only then realized he wasn't aiming for me.

Instead, he cut down Tobias midsentence.

SEVEN

Tobias collapsed without a sound, leaving Armando's knife dripping with blood. Wraithlike, Armando lunged toward me, slashing the blade, reflecting the red-orange light of the performers' sparks.

I threw my hands up in a panic, stumbling backward and taking a gash in my arm from the attack. It *hurt*. It seemed to actually bleed.

I crashed into the hot dog cart, barely noticing as the younger of the two men pulled out his weapon. I didn't care, couldn't care. Armando had become a nightmare. And Tobias . . .

No. Please. Not Tobias.

Ivy cried out, kneeling and trying to help Tobias. Ngozi backed away, horrified.

I reeled.

NOT TOBIAS!

Armando came at me again, and I fled. I pushed off the hot dog cart and ran with my bleeding arm cradled against my chest. Warm liquid soaked through my shirt, wetting my skin. I shoved through the crowd, knocking people over in a wild attempt to stay ahead of Armando.

He flowed after me, more ghost than man or aspect. Obstructions didn't stop him; he passed right through a crowd of people unhindered. He didn't bother to pretend like the others. He didn't need to try to preserve my sanity.

I shoved past a family, scrambling, and somehow got to the front of the crowd, right up near the stage. I'd gotten turned around, confused in my flight.

Red sparks splashed against the wall, then flickered and died. I looked over my shoulder. Radiant, inconsistent, dying light illuminated Armando. His eyes were dead, the eyes of a drowned corpse. He followed, inexorable, brandishing the bloody knife.

"I will cut them out of you," he whispered, voice somehow audible over the sounds of people cheering the show or yelling at me. "I will cut them *all out*."

I collided with someone in the crowd, and they shoved me the other way. My arm protested as I hit another group, and these crushed the wind from me, smashing me between them. Armando flowed through them, his face appearing from someone's back like a stain seeping through a wall.

I screamed again, pushing people away from me, my arm flaring with pain. I squeezed through the stuffy, sweating, screeching, horrible mass. I squirmed and shouted and scrambled and finally . . . I burst from the back of the crowd into open air.

Armando slammed into me from behind, hitting me with his shoulder, throwing me to the ground. I hit the concrete sidewalk and gasped at the pain.

"Cut *them all out*."

I rolled over, and stared up at Armando—who was backlit by an explosion of sparks in the night. He grinned.

Then a bullet took him in the forehead.

He stumbled, shaking his head. More shots followed, like fireworks. Each took him in the face, with almost no spread. He finally collapsed back to the dusty ground, dropping the knife.

I pulled myself away from the corpse, up onto the sidewalk, then twisted about. Never had I been so happy to see J.C. Still holding his sidearm out before him, he stepped over to me and squatted down. "Yup," he said, "a part of me knew I'd have to shoot that guy someday."

I looked back at Armando, lying in an expanding pool of his own blood. J.C. nodded for me to hold my arm out so he could inspect the wound, and I did so, feeling numb.

"So," J.C. said, pulling a bandage from his pocket, "you going to tell me why you were so eager to keep me away?"

"Wha . . . what?"

"Leaving me in a slum, running off from the mansion before I could get back to you. Even my car here got caught in traffic."

"That was real."

"Still feels like you're being reckless. On purpose."

No. I wasn't. I just . . . just wanted to get to Sandra. I tried to explain, but then I felt a *ripping* sensation. Nauseatingly familiar, as it had happened to me earlier today, with Armando. Loss. Information leaving me forever.

This one was much worse. A thunderbolt compared to a twig snapping.

I moaned, huddling into myself, as it left me forever: all the random bits of knowledge that didn't fit into another aspect's expertise.

The trivia that touched everything I did, everything I had learned, wrapped up in a single wonderful man.

Tobias . . .

Tobias was gone.

"What?" J.C. asked. "What is that look on your face, Skinny? What happened?"

"He got Tobias," I croaked.

"Where?" J.C. demanded.

I pointed the way back through the crowd.

J.C. took off running, and I lurched to my feet and followed, leaving Armando's corpse. I didn't *think* it could get up and come after us again . . . but there was no guarantee. Nightmares didn't follow the rules.

By now, the real people had opened a space around me, and backed away as I moved. One got used to this sort of thing in a big city, even if I didn't look like the usual homeless drunk. A few Good Samaritans asked if I needed help, but I managed to brush them off and make my way back toward the hot dog cart.

The two men from earlier had left. Ngozi knelt by Tobias's body, her arms covered in blood. She'd tried, bless her, to bandage him.

It hadn't been enough. J.C. was down on one knee beside Tobias, his handgun held limply. Ivy stood nearby, one arm wrapped around herself while she smoked a cigarette with the other hand. Damn. She'd given that up *years* ago. J.C. rose and walked over to her, and she leaned into him, crying softly on his shoulder.

I just . . .

I stared at the body.

Tobias had been the very first. A calming, optimistic voice pulled from the shadows and nightmares. I remembered sitting at night in a chair, lights off, surrounded by whispers—and then hearing him for the first time.

He had been my lifeline to sanity.

"What . . ." Ngozi said. "What do we do now?"

I didn't know.

"We have to keep moving," J.C. said, still holding Ivy. He needed the comfort as much as she did. "We've drawn attention. Look."

Though the spark show had ended—and someone was starting to spray down the stage with water—security was making its way past the dispersing crowd. A few people turned toward me, gesturing animatedly.

"We can't . . . just leave him," Ivy said.

"There's a way out," I whispered. "A way to fix this. Sandra. She knows." I stumbled over to the hot dog cart. On the counter was a note and the pouch with the cell phone in it. The note read simply, "We'll be in touch."

I grabbed both pouch and note, and—though it pained me to do so—I left Tobias's remains. It felt wrong. It felt awful. I'd come back for him though. I'd give him a proper burial.

He'll just lie there, I thought, *with people walking through him. Never knowing what they're treading on. The great man they could never see, could never know.*

Had to keep moving.

I limped away, still cradling my cut arm as the security guards called after me. They hurried to catch up, but then I approached my limo, which was still parked at the curb.

Barb opened the door, and the two guards backed off. I'd suddenly moved from "random homeless drunk" to "above my pay grade."

I climbed in, then used my foot to kick the door back open as Barb tried to close it after me. Ivy, J.C., then Ngozi entered and slumped into seats.

Barb peeked in. "Um, all in?"

"No," I whispered. "But we can go anyway."

"Sure thing!" she said, chipper. "Anything I can get you? Some water, or—"

"You can shut up."

She closed the door, perhaps a little too firmly. I missed Wilson, and . . .

Oh, hell, *Tobias was dead.*

I lay down on the seat as J.C. knelt by me and worked on the bandage some more.

"Right," Ivy said, taking a deep breath. "Right. We need a plan. I can't believe how much this hurts . . . but we *need a plan*. Steve, this *can't happen again.*"

The car started. Barb flipped on the intercom. "Are we going anywhere specific?"

"No," I said. "Just drive. Please."

Anywhere but here.

EIGHT

I didn't know what type of phone this was.

I turned it over in my hands as the car pulled onto the freeway. Beside me, Ivy helped Ngozi clean the blood off her hands using the limo's sink and water bottles.

Why did it matter what kind of phone it was? Because Tobias had known everything about phones. Not just the devices themselves, but all about the companies that made them. The history of technology was just one of his many little quirks. I'd grown used to having that knowledge comfortably in the back of my brain, not really that important, but still . . . there.

I tried texting Sandra a few times, but she didn't respond. Finally, at a suggestion from J.C., I texted saying I'd turn the phone back on in an hour—then took out the battery, so I couldn't be traced using the phone, just in case.

"J.C.," Ivy said. "Call the mansion."

He did so, dialing Kalyani, then putting her on speaker.

"Is there news?" she asked immediately.

"We . . ." Ivy took a deep breath. "We lost Tobias."

Silence.

"You lost him," Kalyani finally said. "As in . . . he ran away?"

"He's dead," J.C. said. "Gone."

Kalyani gasped.

"We need to prevent something like this from happening again," Ivy said. "I want you to gather all the aspects and get them into the White Room. Let us know if *anyone* is unaccounted for."

"Yes. Yes, okay," Kalyani said. "But . . . Tobias. Are you *sure*?"

"Yes, unfortunately."

"How is Mr. Steve?"

Ivy looked at me. "Not well. Call us back when everyone is together." She hung up.

I stared straight ahead, numb, feeling only the motion of the car on the road.

Get to Sandra.

But would she be able to do anything? Her voice on the line, the way she'd spoken, hadn't sounded like someone who had the answers. Not the right ones, at least.

It was something to think about other than Tobias. Looking up, I was startled to find my aspects all frozen. Like statues, not moving, not breathing. As I realized it, they jerked into motion again, Ngozi drying her hands and telling J.C. about the two men from the hot dog cart.

I checked my phone, and saw that half an hour had passed while I'd sat there, zoned out, thinking about Sandra and Tobias.

The phone buzzed. It was Kalyani calling me.

"Hello," I said, switching it to speaker.

"Everyone is accounted for, Mr. Steve," Kalyani said. "Nobody has vanished. We're all here. Even Leroy, who just got back."

That meant no more nightmares. For now.

"What do you want us to do?" Kalyani asked.

I looked at Sandra's phone. Did we just wait for her, or that Kyle fellow, to "be in touch"? Or did I do something more?

"Options?" I said, looking at my team.

"The older man," Ivy said, "Kyle, he sounded like he was a business type. Not security. So . . ."

"So maybe there's a record of him, and where he works," I said, nodding. "But we'll need a way to search him out. Ngozi. How's your mental image of him?"

"Excellent," she said.

"Great. Kalyani, you still there?"

"Yup."

"Grab Turquoise."

Turquoise was one of my older aspects. He came on, speaking with a weird mix of a Texas accent and a stoner drawl. "Hey, man. This has been crazy, huh?"

"Don't use that word lightly around me, Turquoise," I said. "Ngozi is going to describe someone to you. Can you draw him?"

"Sure. Like one of those guys. From those shows."

"Exactly."

"Cool."

I nodded to Ngozi, who started describing Kyle. Round face, thinning hair, big forearms—like he worked out—but not really an athletic build. Big nose.

Kalyani turned the phone to video mode and showed what Turquoise was drawing. Ngozi coached him to make tweaks, with some input from Ivy, and he did a remarkable job. My brain could memorize complex details quickly. We just needed a way to get the information out.

"Cool," Turquoise said when we were done. "Kind of looks like a potato who is pretending to be a man, and is worried someone will call his bluff."

"You're a weird dude, Turquoise," I said.

"Yeah. Thanks."

"Hey, Chin?" I asked. "You listening?"

"Here," my computer expert said, leaning down and waving into the camera.

"Can you run that sketch through some kind of facial recognition software?" I asked.

"No, but I can tell you who he is anyway."

"What? Really?"

"Sure," Chin said. "I read an article on him recently—that's Kyle Walters, a local entrepreneur. He's made a few waves in local tech circles."

I frowned, Googling the name. "Kyle Walters. President of Walters and Ostman Detention Enterprises."

". . . Detention Enterprises?" Ngozi asked. "Like, prisons?"

"For-profit prisons," Chin said, reading. "He made news by purchasing a game company. It was a moderately big deal in some circles."

I nodded slowly. Whatever Chin knew came from me. I must have read about Kyle during one of my many information binges, where I tried to absorb as many news stories and articles as possible, for future reference.

"Video games and prisons?" Ivy said. "That's an odd pairing."

"Yeah." I scrolled up on the article. "President of the company. Why did he bother coming to meet me himself?"

"Meeting you is quite the experience," Chin said. "He's said to be a hands-on type. Guess he just wanted to see you for himself."

I frowned, studying the article.

"What?" Ivy asked.

"Nothing," I said. "I just . . . I think I used to know something about that structure he's standing in front of." I glanced at the caption below the picture. "'Eiffel Tower'? Looks like some kind of art installation."

"Yeah. A big one." Ivy shook her head. "Strange."

"That's 'art'?" J.C. said. "Looks like someone forgot to finish the thing."

I sat there, waiting for Tobias to explain it to us, then felt again like I'd been punched. He was gone. I took a deep breath and did some further searching into our Kyle Walters fellow. I found some clips of him talking at tech conferences, giving speeches full of buzzwords.

But he owned *prisons*. What was he doing at these conferences? They weren't even security conferences. *Applied Virtual Reality Summit*, I read. Huh.

"He's based locally?" I asked. "Where?"

"Here," Ivy said, showing me her phone, with an address listed. "He owns an entire building in a suburban office park." It appearing on her phone meant I had that address tucked in the back of my brain somewhere, from when I'd memorized local business lists. So I hadn't lost everything with Tobias.

"You seem to be coping remarkably well," Jenny said, "now that the initial shock has worn off. Can you explain how your aspects are helping you to recover?"

Startled, I looked up. There she was, sitting across from me in the limo. J.C., with wonderful presence of mind, pulled his gun and leveled it right at her head.

"Is that necessary?" she asked.

"We just had an aspect go crazy and kill one of my best friends," J.C. said. "I *will* blow the back of your head across that seat if I think it will save anyone else."

"You're not following the rules," I said to her. "Appearing and vanishing? That's dangerous. Nightmares don't follow the rules."

She pursed her lips, and for the first time seemed to *get* that idea. She nodded, and J.C. looked at me.

"You can put it away," I said to him. "She's obviously not a nightmare. Not yet."

He obeyed, holstering it with deliberation as he leaned back in his seat, still watching her. We made fun of J.C., but I'll admit he can be casually intimidating when he really wants to be. Ivy settled in next to him, legs crossed, staring daggers at Jenny. Ngozi had missed the entire exchange, because she was suddenly fixated on how dirty the inside of the cupholder was.

"It seems to me," Jenny said, "that you all are very quick to point a gun—but very slow to ask the difficult questions."

"Such as?" I asked.

"Such as *why* is this happening?" Jenny asked. "*Why* are you losing aspects? What is causing your hallucinations to behave in this way?"

"My brain is overworked. Too many aspects, too much going on with them. Either that or I'm emotionally incapable of handling change in my life."

"False dichotomy," Jenny said. "It could be a third option."

"Such as?"

"You tell me. I'm just here to listen."

"You realize," I said to her, "that I *already* have a psychologist aspect." I nodded toward Ivy. "She gives me lip, but she's good at her job, so I don't need another."

"I'm not a psychologist," Jenny said. "I'm a biographer." She wrote some things in her notepad, as if to prove the point.

I looked out the window, watching streetlights pass on the side of the road. We'd pulled off the freeway, and were heading down a dim neighborhood street. The patches between the lights were dark—almost like nothing existed, except where those streetlights created the world.

I pushed the intercom button. "Barb, GPS an office building called Walters and Ostman Detention Enterprises. Should be on 206th. Take us there."

"Roger, boss," she said.

"Tell me, Mr. Leeds," Jenny said. "Do you want to be cured?"

I didn't answer.

"Say you'd lose us all," Jenny said. "No more aspects. No more knowledge. No more being special. But if you could be normal, would you take that trade?"

When I didn't answer immediately, Ivy shot me a betrayed look. But what could I say? To be well.

To be *normal*.

I did everything I could to remain sane, to shove my psychoses off onto the aspects. I was the most boring of the lot, by design. That way I could pretend. But did that mean . . . mean that I'd welcome losing the aspects?

Could I really live without them?

"I miss Tobias already," J.C. said softly. "He'd have broken this silence. Said something to make me smile."

"Tell me about him," Jenny said. "I barely got to meet him."

It felt like she was trying to worm her way in, dig information from my brain.

"He was wonderful," Ivy said. "Calm with everyone. Interested in everyone."

"He loved a mystery," Ngozi added. "He loved *questions*. He was the part of us that kept wanting to learn."

"I swear," I noted, "half the aspects exist because he was interested enough to get me digging into some strange topic."

"He hated charging people for our work," J.C. said. "Always wanted to give everyone a pro bono deal. Terrible businessman. Good *man* though."

"He was crazy in his own wonderful way," Ivy said. "Remember how people would get when they found out that one of your hallucinations had *his own* hallucination?"

I smiled. Maybe . . . maybe I could imagine Stan, Tobias's astronaut friend. I didn't usually have that much control.

The others continued to reminisce, telling stories about Tobias. Jenny sat back, writing it all down. And it did feel better to talk about it. To remember. Maybe for once she'd actually helped.

Eventually we pulled up to a small business building—maybe four stories high. I didn't know if Sandra was inside, but hopefully they'd at least have information on where she was being held.

I just had to break in and steal it.

∏ I ∏ Ε

"Same car," Ngozi said, peering through the binoculars out the window of our limo. "Big silver SUV that was parked on the street near the hot dog cart. I can barely make out the license plate by the streetlights." She hesitated. "Anyone heard of a 'Lexus' make of cars?"

The aspects shook their heads. How many more aspects could I lose before I was just . . . gone? A drooling vegetable?

J.C. waved for the binoculars, and Ngozi wiped them down with a disinfecting wipe, then passed them over. He looked over the building. "No way to guess at their security level. Here's what we do: We go back to the house and I gather a team of specialized aspects. Chin, Lua, Marci.

"We work some contacts, grab the architectural plans—and, if we're lucky, find out who installed this building's security. We might be able to find out who owned the building before this Kyle guy bought it, and—if they can be bribed—get an even better idea of what we're dealing with. We come back in two days' time, at three in the morning, when . . ."

I opened the door and stepped out into the night.

". . . or not," J.C. said, with a loud sigh.

I knocked on the driver's window, which Barb rolled down. "Go park the car someplace out of sight," I said, then started out toward the office building.

J.C., Ivy, Ngozi, and Jenny followed me. We crossed the dark lawn in a low run. Most parts of the building were floodlit, but on the east side the floodlight was flickering, mostly dark. So I approached from that side.

Jenny hung back the farthest, looking awkward as she tried to hide behind a tree. At least she was playing by the rules now. Ivy had done this sort of thing before, and crept beside J.C. and me with her shoes— not the most practical for an infiltration—held in her hand. I was worried most about Ngozi, but she was smiling as she settled in beside me near some shrubs.

"It's been a while," she whispered as we crouched down in the darkened shadow of the shrubbery. "I feel . . . I feel *good*. Like I can do this. Huh. Oh! Don't brush those leaves! Do you know what kinds of *chemicals* they spray on these things to keep them looking this green?"

J.C. scanned the side of the building. "You insist on doing this now?"

"If Sandra is in there, I want to know. We can't wait two days while they might move her."

He shared a look with Ivy, who shrugged, then nodded.

He breathed out. "You people are all crazy."

"Hey!" Ivy said. "I'm the psychologist here. I get to define who is crazy, and only four of us are."

J.C. counted the five of us. Then, hesitantly, pointed at himself.

"J.C.," she said flatly, "you're as crazy as they come. How many gun magazine subscriptions do you have?"

". . . All of them," he admitted.

"In how many languages?"

". . . All of them."

"And how many of those languages other than English do you read?"

". . . None of them." He peered through the bushes with his binoculars. "But I can read the pictures. Those aren't in Canadian or whatever, eh."

"Who's the sane one, then?" I asked Ivy. "Me?"

"Heavens no. It's Ngozi. Have you *seen* the chemicals they spray on these plants? You should really listen to her."

Ngozi nodded in agreement, but J.C. just chuckled. And I . . . I smiled a little. It was hard to feel any levity after what had happened, but I realized I still needed it.

Thank you, Ivy. "So how do we get in?" I asked.

"Air ducts?" Ngozi asked.

J.C. rolled his eyes. "Have you ever *actually* seen an air duct that a person could climb through? Like, one that was both big enough *and* wouldn't collapse from the weight of a person inside?"

"Sure," she said. "I've seen lots. On TV."

"Yeah, well, how about next time we're doing crime scene analysis, I yell 'enhance' like a billion times."

"Point taken."

"Fortunately," J.C. said, holding up the binoculars again, "this place doesn't look *too* secure. I don't see any external cameras—they could easily be hidden, mind you—and no lights in the windows indicates that if they're patrolling on foot, they're doing so rarely. Of course, these modern joints don't *need* patrols—everything is wired to go crazy the moment you breathe on the wrong door.

"Best way in is to do what Audrey always says—look for the human error, rather than trying to break the machines." He pointed, and I spotted a window on the first floor that had been propped open with a book, perhaps for fresh air.

"We go all at once," J.C. said. "If they're watching the area via camera, stringing it out is worse. This way, at least there's a chance the security guard will be looking away at the moment we run. Ready?"

We each nodded.

J.C. thumbed over his shoulder toward Jenny, who observed from farther back—perhaps not trusting herself to get close. "And her?"

"Ignore her," I said. "She . . . won't show up on their screens. She, um, has a stealth system."

"Not the writer chick," J.C. said, rolling his eyes. He pointed again. "*Her.*"

I looked again. Barb was scuttling across the grass. She arrived, out of breath, and crouched next to me. "All right!" she said. "Sneaking in? I can dig that. What do you want me to do?"

"Go back to the car."

"But—"

"Go back to the car, drive off, and go to your uncle's birthday party. That's happening tonight, right? Grab some cake, Barb."

"You'll need—"

"I'll get a cab. Go."

Her face fell, then she nodded and slunk off. *If she exposed me to the security guards in there* . . . I shook my head, glancing back at the team—and was met with uniform looks of disapproval.

"What?" I said. "We don't need real people."

"There are things she could do that we can't," Ngozi said.

"I'm never one to turn away someone with a can-do attitude," J.C. said.

Ivy just squeezed my arm. "What if that's the problem, Steve? What if you *can't* just live with us? What if turning inward is what's causing all of this?"

"What? You're *that* offended because I turned my *chauffeur* away?" They *were* all crazy.

Besides. Maybe I didn't want someone watching as I went through . . . whatever was happening to me. Can't a man suffer a breakdown in private?

"Let's go," I said—then didn't give them a chance to object as I ran for the building. The others followed, even Jenny. I reached the side of the building, puffing, then approached the open window. It was the type that slid up and down, and through the glass I saw what looked like a service closet. There were buckets on the floor, and it smelled faintly of cleaning fluids. Perhaps they'd been airing it out.

I pulled up the window, then slipped through. I managed to do it without making any noise or knocking over the buckets on the ground, though I bumped my head on a shelf in the dark room as I stood up. I saw stars, and my vision flashed, but I managed to keep myself from shouting out.

I held open the window for the others, and J.C. gave me a thumbs-up as he climbed in. He probably hadn't seen me knock my head, but I figured I was doing better than I might once have. Our training sessions were proving good for something.

Ivy *did* knock over one of the buckets, but fortunately, the resulting clatter wouldn't be audible to anyone but me—though she shot me a chagrined look after doing it. J.C. helped Ngozi in, then Jenny came last.

I replaced the book, rested the window on it, then moved to the door. I took a deep breath and cracked it open. If they had the doors alarmed, this would reveal me.

The light beyond the door was much brighter than I expected. I blinked against the garish, sterile glare. The hallway seemed empty, though J.C. pointed upward to a little knob on the ceiling, a hemisphere of reflective black glass. Security camera.

I pulled back into the room and closed the door with a click. After thinking a moment, I dialed Kalyani on the phone. "Grab Chin," I said softly.

A moment later, he was on the line. "Yeah, boss?"

"We're infiltrating the Detention Enterprises place," I said. "We've breached the perimeter, but the hallways have some surveillance cameras."

Chin chuckled softly. "You're surprised that a group that runs *prison facilities* has a basic level of security?"

"He's been reckless lately," J.C. said. "More so than usual."

"All right. Well, have a look at your phone, boss. You see an app called SAPE? That's your signal analysis booster. Give it a try, and set the thing to transmit data to my laptop."

"Done," I said, flicking a few buttons, watching data appear on my screen.

"Hm . . ." Chin said. "Visible guest wi-fi . . . hidden internal signals not broadcasting identities . . . Okay, cool. They're using AJ141 wireless cameras."

"That's good?"

"Kind of," Chin said. "So those little camera nodes broadcast signals back to a central watch station, right? And the night watchperson there cycles through the cameras."

"Can you hack it?"

"Nope," Chin said. "Not a chance. We'd need to plug into the thing directly, which—if you hadn't guessed—would *kind of* involve going into its field of view. *However,* watch the signal on your phone. See that little blip?"

"Yeah. What is it?"

"That's a ping for data, which is causing the camera to reset briefly and start transmitting. Awkward. They probably configured new cameras to work with their older security setup. It means that while you can't hack the system . . ."

"We *can* see when one of the cameras is transmitting," I said, smiling. "Nice work, Chin."

"Yeah, well, don't get caught, all right? We've had enough bad news today."

"Speaking of that . . ." Kalyani said from near Chin, her voice timid. "Mr. Steve?"

"What?" I said, feeling cold.

"Lua is gone."

"I thought you said you had everyone!"

"We thought we had, but he ran out to grab something from his little survivor hut out back. And he didn't come back! We sent four people out together looking for him, but he's gone."

I leaned back against the wall, feeling sick. No. *Not again . . .*

"Hey Achmed?" J.C. said to Kalyani, leaning down to the phone.

"Please don't call me that."

"Yeah. Sorry. Trying to be funny, you know . . ." He took a deep breath. "There's a key hidden in a box under the third brick on the back path. Go grab it."

"For what?" Kalyani asked.

"It opens my gun locker, the one in the main hallway, where I keep the emergency shotguns in case of home invasion. Distribute them among the others, and you guys hole up in there, okay? Stay in one room, barricade the door . . . and be careful. If Lua goes nightmare, he might ignore things like locks and barricades. Guns should still work though."

"I . . ." Her voice trembled. "Okay. Okay, we'll do it."

"Good. Take care." He looked up at me, uncharacteristically reserved, then unholstered his sidearm. "Guess you were right, Skinny. Waiting two days to get in here wasn't an option."

"Do you want to tell me," Jenny said from right beside me, "how exactly this makes you feel?"

I jumped, and suddenly felt an irrational anger at her. She stood there, scribbling, like she didn't even *care* what was happening to everyone else.

"Either you are going to shut up," I said, "or we are going to come to blows."

"False dichotomy," she said. "There are more than two options. We could—"

"Go," I said, pointing back at the window.

"What?" she said, lowering her pad.

"Go. *Now.* Or I swear, J.C. will shoot you. Break the rules, get away, vanish—I don't care how. But *go away!*"

She vanished in a heartbeat.

I trembled inside, then felt sick. The other aspects stood silently. "Don't look so betrayed," I snarled. "I didn't ask for her. I didn't want her. I don't even know what kind of specialty she was supposed to represent."

I waited for the camera outside to go through a cycle, counting how long we had between its bursts. A minute and a half. Plenty of time.

J.C. led the way out into the hallway.

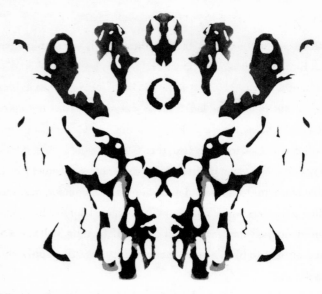

T E Π

The cameras were spaced evenly through the hallways, but with my phone, I was able to pick out the closest signals. I got into a good rhythm, delaying underneath one camera while it was still offline, then quickly moving when the next one stopped transmitting. I tried doorknobs as I passed, hoping to find one unlocked that would provide computer access.

I didn't have luck at that, but Ngozi did spot something through the window into one office: a map of the facility on the back wall. I snapped a picture, then found my way to a spot around a corner and at the landing of a stairwell where we thought we'd be out of sight of the two nearest cameras.

Here, I took a breather while my aspects gathered around the phone to inspect the map. My heart was beating quickly, and my shirt was damp with nervous sweat. But so far, no alarm.

That doesn't mean anything, I reminded myself. *Any alarm would be silent, only alerting security.* Still, this entire place seemed eerily quiet. Empty, but bright, lit up white.

"There," J.C. said, pointing at the picture of the map, with its breakdown of four floors. One larger bit of text read: *Subject testing and holding cells.*

"What you want to bet she's in there?" J.C. asked.

I nodded. We went up the stairwell—dodging a camera in the middle of the next flight—and ended up on the top floor, near those holding cells. Here, unfortunately, we encountered our first live guards. I peeked around a corner, and found them right in the hallway. They leaned against the wall, tasers on their hips, chatting softly about football.

I backed away, looking down the corridor behind me, but the map said that direction only led to a dead end at a place labeled IMAGING CENTER.

I retreated to the top of the stairs, in a spot out of sight of the cameras. "Ideas?" I whispered to my aspects.

"You could take two guards," J.C. said.

Fat chance of that.

"I doubt we can talk past them," Ivy said, "considering the circumstances."

"Well," Ngozi said. "There's an air duct over there, down that hallway to the left."

"Not that again," J.C. said. He squinted. "We wouldn't fit."

"I wasn't thinking of going into it ourselves. . . ."

I waited, nervously, hidden on the steps and barely daring to breathe as kitten sounds echoed in the hallway above.

It took only a few minutes for the two men to approach, leaving their post. Confused, they passed right near my stairwell, then continued on down the hallway, turning left. They probably shouldn't have left their posts, but it was perfectly natural. Who *wouldn't* be interested by the sounds of a lost kitten?

They'd find the sounds coming from the air duct where we'd hidden—around a corner and out of sight—Sandra's phone, playing the meowing kitten video that Audrey had been watching earlier. It had been dangerous turning on Sandra's phone, but we'd put it into airplane mode and used a direct Bluetooth connection between my phone and it to load the cat video.

I heard the men in the corridor nearby, calling to the kitten in the air duct. I slipped past them, around the corner. Heart pounding, I walked underneath a sign that read, SECURE AREA—SUBJECT HOLDING. Just a little farther. Sandra. I heard . . . I heard her voice ahead. Singing. That old lullaby that she always—

Everything flashed white.

The hallway melted into light. I stumbled, and J.C. shouted, raising his gun and spinning around. For a moment, we were blinded.

The light vanished, and I found myself in a completely different place. Instead of the hallway, I was lying on the floor in an unfamiliar room. It was a large, open chamber with concrete walls, a high ceiling, and industrial lighting.

What had happened? I'd . . . been teleported, somehow?

Kyle Walters stood before me: the balding, somewhat buff man in the sport coat from earlier at the fairgrounds. I blinked, looking up at him, then at the small gathering of techy types behind him. Where had they come from? What was happening?

"Welcome, Mr. Leeds," he said, "to the future of human incarceration."

ELEUEN

Kyle offered a hand to help me to my feet. He had a false sort of friendliness about him, the smile of a man who would be your best friend for as long as it took to sell you a very nice pre-owned vehicle.

My surroundings had gone from a sterile hallway to an older warehouse. Not dingy, but *used*. Concrete floors with patches covered with chunks of carpet where computer stations had been set up. The scents were no longer of cleaning fluids, but of sawdust and someone's microwave dinner. It wasn't messy, it was just . . . real?

Real. That other building had been too perfect, maybe even too generic. The kind of tech office that you saw people infiltrate in films. A too-perfect, constructed world. Hadn't Chin said this man had bought a video game company?

But how had he made me feel like I was there? I wasn't wearing any equipment. "What did you do to me?" I asked.

"I took you to the *future*, Steve!" Kyle obviously wasn't the type of person who asked before using your first name. "You did pretty well."

"We haven't ever seen the trick with the cat sounds," said one of the techs behind him, a woman with her hair in a ponytail. "Innovative."

"You found the camera exploit as well," another one said. "So far, only security professionals have done that. Everyone else tries something cliché like taping a picture of the hallway in front of the camera."

"How did you do it, though?" I asked. "I'm not wearing a headset or anything. How did you put me into that virtual world?"

"We prefer the term 'holodeck,'" one of the techies said.

"No we don't," Kyle said quickly. "Ignore them. We prefer a proprietary term that carries no legal baggage or IP infringement." He slapped me on the shoulder, then put his arm around me.

Nearby, J.C. pointed out two men hanging back near a wall. One was the other guy from the hot dog stand, and both were packing nine-millimeters.

"I don't like this at all," Ivy said. "So everything we did . . . the incursion, dodging the cameras . . . it wasn't real?"

Neither are you, I thought. *Neither is most of my life.*

"You're turning VR into . . . prisons?" I asked Kyle.

"The natural response to current market incentives," Kyle said, steering me along as he started walking. "Here, let me unpack it for you. Do you know how much it costs to house an inmate in the United States for a year?"

"It's high," I said. "Like, twenty or thirty—"

"It costs an average of thirty thousand dollars!" Kyle said. "And can get as high as *sixty thousand* in some states. Per year, *per inmate*! And what do we, the taxpayers, gain from all of that? Are the inmates at least well cared for? No! Criminal-on-criminal violence is rampant. Living conditions are terrible. Prisons are overfilled, understaffed, and underfunded. In short, we're spending a ton for a cruddy product. How smart is that?"

"The solution seems to be to make sure fewer people go to prison."

"A wonderful ideal, Steve! I'm glad we have people like you to deep dive into the morality of situations. But for the real world, we also need people like me—and a little *practical* application."

"You still haven't told me how you immersed me in one without my knowledge."

Kyle led me to a window that looked in on a small room where a man lay in a bunk, peacefully asleep. Ivy and Ngozi crowded around. J.C. was playing it cool, standing back, glaring at those security guards.

"Emitters on the ceiling," Kyle said, pointing upward. "We can engage them without the subject knowing they're transitioning into a virtual world. That's the key; if they think it's real, all *kinds* of possibilities open up. This is the future, Steve. This changes the paradigm. It digs up the goalpost, and moves it to a completely different game."

I looked back through the window, feeling sick.

"Right now," Kyle said, "that man is working on an elaborate escape plan from the prison room he *thinks* he's in. We've offered carefully calculated goals—manageable hooks he can exploit to get him closer and closer to escaping. He's *engaged*, he's *excited*. He thinks he's going to do it—and in the meantime, we're paying the equivalent of less than *ten thousand* a year to keep him in there."

"Calculated goals," I said. "Like what?"

"Our basic prison plan will offer a multitude of potential escape routes," one of the techs said. "We're working on a tunneling quest line, a quest line involving the befriending of guards, and a third that involves escaping using the laundry bins. Or if the prisoner prefers, they will be able to become kingpin of the prisoners—gaining dominance over the various factions, and eventually moving into a suite within the facility to live like a king."

"What about muscle atrophy?" Ivy asked. "Bedsores? I can think of a dozen problems with this."

I repeated the objections, and Kyle just grinned. "You're a smart cookie, Steve," he said. "We're working on these issues—we have emitters that let the body move while the brain thinks it's in the real world. Ideally, we'll be able to use a mixture of idle and physical interaction to create a sustainable, perpetual, eco-friendly, and health-conscious incarceration solution."

"A video game for inmates."

"That and so much more! In our simulated routines, the prisoners have as much as a tenfold increase in satisfaction. Yes, game companies have been pioneering this technology—but nobody has been asking the most important question."

"Which is?"

"How can we get the government to sink a *ton* of money into this?" Kyle grinned. He seemed to do that a lot. "Incarceration is such a nasty business to the public. They don't want to think about it. They don't want to interact with it. Nobody wants a prison in their back yard, but everybody wants 'those people' to be taken care of. Well, we can take care of them."

Kyle rapped the window with the back of his hand. "For now, we can only simulate a simple prison facility, but we have plans. What if a prisoner could escape into the virtual world, but not know they're in a simulation? We could watch and see if they go back to a life of crime. If they do . . . well, we let them live in their own world of vice, hurting nobody. But if it turns out they have rehabilitated, or might have been innocent all along, we can just let them out. It's a *perfect* system."

"It's fake," I whispered.

"And which would you rather live in? The fake prison where you think you're free, or the real prison where you spend each day in drudgery? Honestly, when this project goes live, people will be *begging* to be let in."

"Yet something's wrong, isn't it?" Ivy said, narrowing her eyes and reading Kyle. "Ask him why he needs you."

"If it's so great, why kidnap Sandra?"

"Kidnap? Steve, Sandy came to us. And she suggested that we approach you."

"You could have sent me a letter."

"We sent seven."

I hesitated. Seven?

"Maybe we should answer our mail once in a while," J.C. said. "You know, for old times' sake."

Kyle cleared his throat. "We tried working through contacts to get your attention, we tried calling, we even sent Gerry by to knock on your door."

"You weren't 'taking new clients,'" the tech said. "I couldn't get past the gate."

It *had* been a while since I'd taken a case. The house staff had orders to turn away supplicants.

I stepped up close to the window, looking in at the prisoner. Lying there, eyes closed, asleep. But awake somewhere else. "Is Sandra in one of these rooms?"

"She is. But let's not get to that yet. You asked what's wrong with our system—and well, there *are* a few bugs. Turns out, human brains are *very* good at picking out when things are wrong. There are so many details to get right—and the processing power needed to simulate reality is enormous. We do a poor job, and the imperfections build up. Normal people last maybe a few hours in the simulation, depending on their brain chemistry."

"The brain eventually rejects the reality," the woman tech said. "Much as it might reject a transplanted organ."

"The whole thing collapses," Kyle said. "They come out of it, and we can't get the simulation to take for them again until two or three days have passed." He paused. "Sandy's record in the simulation so far is eighty-seven consecutive days."

J.C. whistled softly.

"She got kicked out again this morning," one of the techs said, "and went on a little jaunt to the fairgrounds to contact you. Wanted to do it in person. Once she spoke to you earlier, she asked to go back in. It took for her immediately. It always does."

"Somehow," Kyle said, "her brain can make up for the gaps in our programming. We can transmit *concepts* to Sandy, and she makes up the rest, adding in the details. We need to figure out how she does this, because it could be the key. If we can get the brains of our subjects to construct their own reality, we don't need to re-create things exactly—we can just nudge them the direction we want, and let their minds do the hard work."

"You're the same way," a techie noted. "We turned on the simulation the moment you climbed in through the window, and your brain blurred the real reality into our fake one, filling in details that we got wrong, or that were too low resolution. Your brain, quite frankly, is *amazing*."

I rubbed my head, remembering when I'd bumped it into that shelf while climbing in the window. My vision had flashed white. Had that been the moment?

Ngozi had wandered over to the nearest of the computer stations, and was looking over the equipment—but I wasn't sure what we'd be able to tell without Chin here. Hell, this might be out of even his league. Wirelessly projecting global hallucinations directly into the brain? That was some Arnaud "theoretical physics" levels of science.

I looked to the side, to get Tobias's read on the situation. But there was no Tobias. Not anymore.

"So they need our brain," Ivy said. "You can make your own reality, Steve, and they want to know how."

"But they already have Sandra," I said. "Why do they need me?"

"Try understanding a disease with only one patient," Kyle said. "Or doing a drug test with only one subject. You're an incredibly rare find, Steve. Your mind is worth *millions*. All we want is for you to spend some time in the simulation. A few years at most."

A few *years*?

"No chance," I said. "I'm already wealthy. What could you possibly offer me to live in your box?"

"Sandra is free of her aspects," Kyle said.

Ivy looked at me sharply.

Kyle smiled. "You're interested, I see. Yes, she asked if we could stop the hallucinations. Construct a reality where she was free of them." He hesitated, and I caught what I thought was a sign of discomfort from him. "It . . . didn't work like we thought it would."

"When we put her into the simulation," a techie said, "she *added* to the programming, making her aspects appear. And they interacted with the world we created—Sandra layered another reality on top of our virtual reality, and adapted the code. But she wanted the aspects gone . . . and turns out, we could help with that."

I shivered. Something about the tone in his voice.

"Anyway," Kyle said, "Sandy's been very helpful. She's showing us how the brain alters its own reality. We aren't really sure exactly why or how our programs interact with her aspects, but they do—we're getting all kinds of interesting interactions between our tech and her brain. One thing is certain. We can help you be free of them, like she is. No more aspects—no more nightmares. No more voices."

Ivy looked aghast. J.C., though, met my eyes and nodded. He'd never wanted to be an aspect. He could understand how part of me just wanted things to be . . . normal.

"Let me talk to Sandra," I said.

Kyle winced. "Now, see, here's the problem. She's my only chip in this particular bet. Surely you see I can't give her up without something in return? Look, let's do a quick deal. Handshake. Give me a few days of data, and let me prove to you that I can create a reality where you don't have aspects. In turn, I'll let you talk to Sandra."

"He's a snake, Steve," Ivy said. "I can't believe you're even *considering* this. Why are we listening?"

I closed my eyes. But it *was* strangely tempting. Last time I'd tried to get away, Joyce had come complaining that I never took her on missions, Armando had phoned me seventeen times, and I'd found Ivans in the closet drinking the bottle of hotel wine. On top of it all, J.C. had shown up "just in case."

My life was so stuffed full of fake people, I didn't have room for anything or anyone else. But that look in Ivy's eyes. And this offer . . . it would only give me another layer of fakeness. I wouldn't be normal, because none of it would be real.

"No deal," I said, turning to walk away. My three aspects joined me as I strode toward the front door of the large, hollow room.

"Very well," Kyle said with a sigh. "Gerry, try the isolation program on him."

I spun. "You can't—"

"Steve, *you* broke into *my* offices. *You're* the trespasser. I'm perfectly justified in holding you a little while, to be certain you aren't dangerous. Until the authorities arrive." He smiled. "Next time, maybe don't screw with the guy who literally owns the prison."

I lunged for him, but the room flashed white.

I stumbled over a rock and hit the ground. A sandy beach, with waves softly lapping to my right, a jungle to my left. My aspects stumbled around, J.C. with hand on gun, Ngozi gasping—horrified—to be suddenly outdoors someplace so wild.

A deserted island.

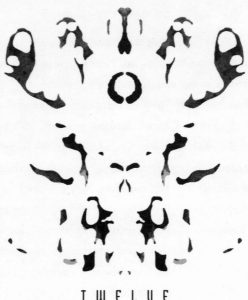

T W E L V E

"That rat!" J.C. shouted. "That *slimeball*. He's getting free time study-ing us!"

Ivy helped me to my feet, but I had difficulty meeting her eyes. I sat down on a rock by the water, feeling exhausted. I was so *tired*. Tired of being a test subject. Tired of imagining a world where everyone lived—had friends, fell in love, visited family—except me.

Tired of being the middle manager of my own existence.

"I can't believe this!" J.C. shouted. "I can't . . . Yo, Ngozi. You okay?"

She shook her head. "No. This is *horrible*. Where are my gloves?" She fished in her pockets.

"Yeah," J.C. said, "but—like—there's no people, right? So no germs."

"Except for the fact that we're not really on a beach!" she said. "We're in that smelly warehouse, next to a table full of *six* old Chinese delivery containers. I'm going to end up touching one by accident."

"So what do we do?" Ivy looked toward J.C.

"Don't look at me," he said. "All I know how to do is shoot people and make clever wisecracks."

"Oh *please*," Ivy said. "Your wisecracks are *not* clever."

I put my head in my hands, looking at a wave roll in, feeling a pounding headache come on.

"I think Steve is going to be indisposed for a little while," Ivy said. "We might need to solve this ourselves. Ngozi, ideas?"

"Well, there are footprints in the sand over there," she said. "Might be one of those 'quest lines' the tech people were talking about."

I watched the wave roll in, deposit some sand, then die off. It would all just get sucked out again when the tide changed. Then return. A thousand little versions of Sisyphus, repeating until the sand wore away to nothing.

"Steve," Ivy said, stepping up. "We're going to follow those footprints. We'll be back in a minute. You'll be okay?"

I didn't reply.

"Just stay here, all right?"

They walked off. A part of me noticed that they were acting a little strange. They almost never left me. But now they went off exploring?

Maybe, I thought, *maybe they're excited to be able to actually interact with a world. In here, everything is fake. So maybe it's better for them.*

Or . . . was Kyle going to do something to them? To prove he could leave me here alone? How long would he hold me here? How long *could* he?

A strong hand gripped me on the shoulder. I jumped, turning, and found Lua standing behind me. Lua! He'd vanished from the mansion, becoming a nightmare.

I screamed and scrambled off the rock, pulling out of his grip and dropping into the rolling surf. I splashed, climbing to my feet, soaked wet and holding out my phone—for some reason I would never have been able to articulate—as if it were a weapon. Only then did I realize something was wrong. Lua didn't *look* like a nightmare—he didn't have the dead eyes or the sunken face. He looked just like his normal self.

"Sorry, boss. Didn't mean to sneak up on you." The large Samoan man folded his arms. He was wearing jeans and flannel, with the sleeves rolled up. He inspected the sky, then the woods, then the rock I'd been sitting on. "A deserted island. Of all the places for you to end up."

"It's . . . it's not real."

"What is?" he asked, then chuckled. He never laughed loudly, but I'd also never known him to be angry. In fact, it was hard for me to imagine him as a nightmare, like Armando had become.

"They got all the clichés at least," Lua said. "That bay is right out of a freaking Disney movie, complete with—yes—the mast of a sunken ship. Tribal drums in the background. Mysterious footprints. What you want to bet that if we start digging, we'll find a treasure chest somewhere on this beach?" He started toward the woods. "Well, let's get you out of here."

"Out?" I asked, scrambling across the beach behind him. "How?"

"They implied earlier they couldn't re-create more than a small space," he said. "A building at most. So I figure, if we get you out into the water—away from the actual island—the thing will fall apart." He started pulling at some vines dangling from a tree.

"Lua?" I said. "How do you know what they said to me earlier? You weren't there."

"I know what you know, boss. And you know what I know."

"It doesn't work that way."

"Why?"

"Because," I said. "Because that's the way I stay sane. That's the way Sandra set it up."

Lua grunted. "How did that work out for her?" He knelt down, twisting the vines to strengthen them, then wrapping them around the edge of a small fallen log.

"Lua, you're breaking the rules. I didn't bring you on this mission."

He kept wrapping the log, affixing it to another log he pulled from the underbrush. "Boss," he said softly, "you need to see what is real."

I stepped back; that was what Armando had said. I reached for a stick to use as a weapon, pulling at it, but it was stuck in the underbrush.

Lua went faintly transparent, as if he weren't all there. "I guess," he said as he worked, "we have different ways of trying to make you confront it. Armando, he always *was* a little loony. He had a loony solution."

I glanced in the direction the others had gone. I *really* didn't want to be alone with a possible nightmare.

"Don't mind them," Lua said. "They're getting pulled into the simulation, you know? Rolling with it." He yanked on his log and pulled—from the underbrush—a fully formed catamaran ship, made of logs and vines. "Not the best I've ever made," he noted, "but it's not bad, considering what I had to work with."

I gaped. That was a *serious* breaking of the rules.

"In here, you *are* the rules, boss." I could still see through him, and got the distinct impression that in his outline—as if he were a window—I could see a concrete floor, some desks with computers.

Voices.

He's up and walking. The brain has stopped suppressing his movement, even when we tell it to. That's new.

How are the readings?

Interesting. Completely different from Sandra—and completely different from when he broke in. These readings mean he's adding aspects into the simulation, though. The program should be able to interact with them, like we interacted with Sandra's aspects.

"I could live here," I said to Lua. "I could let them create my reality, and I could just . . . go with it."

"Isn't that what you do anyway?" He smiled, then turned and waved at the other three, who were walking back along the beach. He gestured toward the boat, looking very proud.

"Lua," I said. "What does it all mean? Why is this happening to me? How do I stop it?"

"You think I know? I'm what you made me to be—the guy who can get you off an island. In the end, we're all just trying to help." He got behind the boat and shoved his weight against it, pushing it along the sand toward the water.

J.C. and Ivy arrived to help push, while Ngozi complained that seawater was "full of animals." Finally she climbed aboard, then J.C. and Ivy joined her—with Lua ready to push the boat the rest of the way out into the water. He waved me toward the last seat in the catamaran.

I stepped into the warm water. "They can just stick me into another VR world if I escape this one."

"Nah," Lua said. "You can see through it."

"That's crazy," I said. "I can't even see what is real in my own *bedroom*."

"And tell me. Who is the strongest, boss? The guy who never goes to the gym, or the guy who tried—but failed—to bench his best yesterday?" He nudged me toward the boat, looking even more transparent than before.

I sat down, then realized there were only four seats. "You're not

coming?"

"Gotta stay here now," he said, giving the boat a good shove. "Broke too many rules. But don't worry about me. I've got a day job." He winked. "Call center for an insurance company. Something boring. *Normal*."

He pushed us out into the water, then waved as we picked up oars and began to row. I watched him as he vanished, and I braced myself for the ripping sensation, the loss of knowledge and information. But this time it was more . . . more like a subtle *fade*. Like falling asleep.

The simulation barely lasted twenty feet beyond the small bay. One second we were rowing, and the next, the four of us were standing back in the warehouse. I reached up, wiping the tears from my eyes.

"That was awful," Gerry—the tech—complained from his seat at the computers. "He didn't follow any of the quest paths. He just broke the thing."

"A ton of hard work, flushed right down the drain," the female techie complained.

"It's the aspects," Kyle said. "They're letting him cheat. We're going to have to remove them. He'll be helpless without them."

"No," I said. "Listen. I—"

"Don't worry, Steve," Kyle said. "They aren't actually people. No loss. Mob scenario, Gerry."

The room flashed white, and we were standing in an old-time casino, next to a spinning roulette wheel.

A man burst through the door. "Big Salamander is here!" he shouted. "He's wise to—"

Gunfire blasted through the door, ripping through the man's body. He collapsed as men flooded into the room, then began shooting people indiscriminately.

THIRTEEN

Ivy fell first. She clung to my arm as she looked at the bullet wound in her stomach. Then she began to slide down.

"No. No, no, no!" I screamed, kneeling beside her. Gunfire tore up the room. Ngozi dove for cover, but a bullet hit her in the forehead, and she collapsed. J.C. kicked over a table, then grabbed Ivy, hauling her behind cover.

I scrambled over beside them, bullets blasting wood chips from nearby tables. People screamed, but for once, J.C. didn't return fire. He pressed his hand against Ivy's wound. "Hey. Hey, stay with us. Ivy?"

"Steve," she whispered. "Steve!"

I huddled beside the overturned table.

"You need to promise," she said to me, "that you won't abandon the rest of them. That you won't let us end like this."

"I promise," I whispered.

She smiled, lips bloody. "That was a lie." She nodded toward J.C., and tried to sit up. He helped her, and then she kissed him. An intimate last kiss, amid a hail of gunfire. Our table wasn't doing much good. A shot went right through the wood and hit J.C. in the shoulder, but he lingered on the kiss until Ivy was gone.

He reverently lowered her body back down onto the floor. Then he looked at me, bleeding from one arm. "You're going to have to handle this alone, Skinny."

"I can't, J.C. I *can't*."

"Sure you can. You had an awesome teacher."

"Don't—"

"Why do you think I've been training you all this time? I knew." He tapped his head. "See what's real. You can do it."

"J.C. . . ."

He raised his fist toward me. "For good luck."

I raised my fist, then tapped his. He grinned, then pulled one gun from a holster under his arm and a second one from a hidden holster strapped to his right ankle. He stood up.

And was hit with about a hundred rounds at once. He collapsed back to the ground without getting off a single shot.

"No!" I screamed. "*NO!*"

I let out a ragged, raw screech, a moan of pain and frustration. Of *anger*. I rocked back and forth on my ankles as the bullets demolished the room. But they didn't hurt me. They weren't real.

Not . . . real.

The shooters grew faintly transparent. The splinters flying off the table, the spilled casino chips, the fallen corpses. It all . . . faded. The roar of the gunfire became a buzzing. In its place, I heard voices.

We need to learn why he's still up and moving.

We could tie him down maybe.

I could see them gathered around, watching me. Shadows looming, all save for one man at a desk of computers. *Chin*, I thought. *I need you.*

I stood up. Then, for effect, I ducked in a low run and scuttled across the casino room, as if trying to dodge bullets. That put me close to the computer desk in the real world.

To my eyes, the virtual casino faded further, and I could see real-world details. Kyle, grinning as if amused to see how helpless I was. The two guards approaching, perhaps worried that I'd hurt myself or ruin something in my thrashing.

The computer monitor.

"Yeah," Chin said in my ear. "That's easy. Not a bad UI, for what has to be an early build."

"Emitters are along the ceiling of this warehouse," Arnaud said. "In the whole room."

"Click that radio button," Chin said, "and change the target from 'single subject' to 'entire room.' See that checked box at the bottom? The one that says 'Debugging mode.' I suggest turning that off, as it might prevent them from using backdoors they've made to get themselves out of the simulation. Good luck."

I leaped for the computer, shoved Gerry aside, and clicked as Chin had instructed.

The guard from the hot dog stand rushed for me, but moved too slowly to stop me. Instantly, we were all there together. Kyle, the two guards, Gerry and the other techies. We stood in that casino, surrounded by dead people. The mobsters had stopped shooting, and were now picking through the wreckage.

"Oh, hell," Gerry said. He scrambled for the now-vanished computer controls, but just waved his hands through empty space. "Oh, *hell!*"

The hot dog guard grabbed me by the arm. "This won't accomplish anything. You're still in our prison."

I sagged in his grip, glancing toward J.C., dead on the floor. I muttered something softly.

"What's that?" the guard said, shaking me by the arm. "What did you say?"

"This isn't your prison," I muttered louder. "It's *mine*."

I bolted upright, slamming the back of my head into the guard's nose. As he shouted in pain I turned, grabbing him by the arm and flipping him over, then slammed him into the ground. I came up with his handgun, and held it out, sighting—flipping off the safety—just as J.C. had taught me.

Thank you.

I squeezed the trigger, firing off three quick shots, bringing down virtual mobsters who had been picking through the room. I wasn't really worried about them, but I wanted to get the others into firing mode. Indeed, the rest of the mobsters raised their weapons and started shooting again.

The other people—one more guard, Kyle, the four techs—screamed and dodged behind overturned tables. "It's not real!" Kyle shouted. "Remember, it's not real!"

It didn't matter. I'd been there so many times. What sounded real, what looked real, *was* real to you—even if you logically knew otherwise. Even Kyle ran for the doorway to a bathroom, where he could hide from the gunfire.

I stalked through the room. A pile of poker chips next to me exploded as a bullet hit. Shots passed right through me. I reached to my arm, where Armando had cut me, and found only smooth, unmarred skin. When had I started ignoring that wound?

A guard—one of the real people—pointed his gun toward me, so I was forced to shoot him in the shoulder. He screamed, and I casually stepped over and kicked his gun away from him. I pushed him down and took a second gun from his leg holster.

Thanks again, J.C.

I stood up and fired in two directions at once, simultaneously killing two mobsters. The techs were screaming somewhere nearby, but the only person I really cared about was hiding in the bathroom. I stepped up to the wall nearby, then pushed through. I didn't break through; I just shoved my way past it. As I did, the virtual world became even more flimsy to my eyes.

In the bathroom, Kyle spun on me, but I easily swept his feet out from under him, stepped on his wrist—getting him to drop the gun—then kicked his weapon away. I leaned down in a smooth motion and pressed two weapons to the sides of his head.

"Two guns, Kyle," I whispered. "One is real, one is fake. Can you tell which is which? Can you feel them, cold against your skin?"

He stared up at me, sweating.

"Death in one hand," I whispered, "a game in the other. Which should I fire? Right or left? Would you like to choose?"

He tried to stammer out some words, but couldn't even form a sentence. He lay there, trembling, until I stood up. Then I casually shot him in the side.

Kyle screamed, doubling over, blood leaking between his fingers.

"I lied, Kyle," I said, tossing the gun away. "Both guns are fake. I got them in the simulation. But you couldn't tell, could you?"

He continued to whimper at the pain.

"Don't worry," I said. "The wound isn't real. So no actual loss. Right?"

I dropped out of the simulation. The six people lay unconscious on the floor, trapped in the simulation. Of my aspects—J.C., Ivy,

Ngozi—there was no sign. Though I did feel a buzz from my phone. A call, from Kalyani.

I didn't answer. A moment later, a text came.

GOODBYE, MISTER STEVE.

Somehow I knew what was happening. Some of them had turned against the others, becoming nightmares. By ordering them all to congregate, I'd simply made the massacre easier. I tucked the phone away, and decided I didn't want to know which of them had chosen that path.

I just knew that when I returned, there wouldn't be any left. It was over.

Exhausted, I strode along the wall and looked into the windows here. Each was a cell, for testing patients.

Sandra was in the last one, seated on a short stool, eyes closed. I checked the wall monitor, tweaked a few settings, then opened the door.

I stepped into Sandra's world.

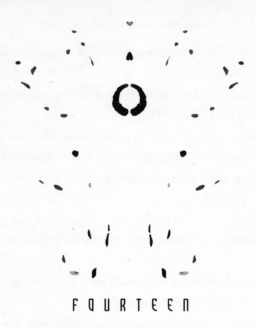

FOURTEEN

Her final hallucination took the form of a long pier at night, extending into a placid sea. Little paper boats with candles at the centers floated along, bobbing and bumping into one another.

They didn't do much to light the sea, but they did contrast with it. Fire upon the water. Frail lights one step from being snuffed out.

I walked along the pier, listening to quiet waves lap against the posts beneath, smelling brine and seaweed. Sandra was a silhouette sitting at the end of the pier. She didn't turn as I settled down next to her.

She was older than I remembered, of course. The older I grew, the more shocking it was to see weathering on the faces of people I'd once known. But she was still Sandra—same long face, same eyes that seemed to be always dreaming. A beautiful sense of control and serenity.

"Do you recognize it?" she asked.

"That place along the coast where we went," I said. "With the buskers on the dock." I could faintly hear jazz music in the distance. "You bought a necklace."

"A little chain. And you bought it for me." She put her hand to her neck, but she wasn't wearing it.

"Sandra . . ."

"It's falling apart, isn't it?" She continued to stare out across the ocean. "You're losing control of them too?"

"Yes."

"I was wrong. When I taught you all those years ago. I thought we could contain it, but we can't. I suppose . . . suppose it doesn't matter. It's all just in our heads."

"Who cares if it's all in our heads?"

Finally she looked at me, frowning.

"*Who cares?*" I said. "Yes, it's all in my head. But pain is 'all in my head' too. Love is 'all in my head.' All the things that matter in life are the things you can't measure! The things our brains make up! Being made-up doesn't make them *unimportant*."

"And if they control your life? Dominate it? Take you away from anything that could be real or lasting?"

I waved toward her simulated world. "This is better?"

"I'm at peace here. For the first time in my life." She hesitated, then met my eyes. "The second time."

"You told me I had to have purpose, Sandra. Is this purpose? Sitting here? Alone?"

"I have no choice," she said, then embraced me. "Oh, Rhone. I tried to leave again today. I visited the fairgrounds, to call you. They came back as whispers. It will happen to you too. They will steal your sanity. Unless you do . . . something . . . to contain them."

The tiny, paper-borne lights trembled on the ocean, and in a moment I caught a glimpse of the dark shallows underneath . . . and dead eyes staring up out of the water.

Sandra held on tighter. I pulled her close as I picked out dozens upon dozens of corpses in the water, entombed in the depths. Her aspects.

"Oh, Sandra," I whispered.

"It is peace. The only peace I'll ever find."

I closed my eyes against that horror. Such loss . . . the agony of feeling pieces inside of you being ripped away. I knew *exactly* what she'd gone through. Likely, I was the only living person who could fully empathize with what she felt.

"Mine are dead too," I whispered.

"Then you can escape."

"And if I don't want to? If I *want* them back?"

"It doesn't work that way. Once they die, they're gone for good. Even if you make new ones, the aspects you had can never return."

We embraced there for . . . I don't know how long. It could have been hours. Finally, I pulled back from her and—looking into her eyes—knew that she didn't have any answers for me. At least not answers I wanted.

There was an indescribable hollowness behind her eyes. I'd heard it in her voice before, on the phone. She'd lost so much, she'd seen so many nightmares. It had led her to this. A terrible numbness. Like a real-life version of becoming a nightmare.

For a brief moment, I saw through the illusion, the hallucination. I was in a small room, and Sandra—it *was* her, alive and real—sat on a little stool on the floor beside me. Though our surroundings were a figment, she was real. She'd always been real. I knew that as well as I knew anything.

"Stay," Sandra said to me.

"All those years ago," I said softly, "when you left me . . . I tormented myself, Sandra. Yet my aspects were never able to solve this one most important mystery. Where had you gone? *Why* had you gone?"

"Rhone . . ." she said. "That doesn't matter now. *Stay.* If we have to be alone, let's be alone together."

"Do you know," I said, ignoring her plea, "a piece of me always suspected that I knew why you'd gone. I'd become too needy. That was the reason, wasn't it? You couldn't keep dealing both with your aspects *and* with my problems."

I stood up to leave, but let her hand linger in mine.

"I think I now understand your decision," I said. "Not why you left . . . but why you *had to* leave. Does that make sense?"

"It will happen faster next time, Rhone," she whispered. "If you go back out—if you claw your way through the whispers and nightmares again—the next set of aspects will degrade quickly. They'll die within months. It happened to me."

I winced, looking away, still holding her hand.

"It's either stay here in peace," Sandra said, "or go out there and suffer."

False dichotomy.

"And is there no third option? A path between the two?"

"No."

"You're wrong." I dropped her hand and turned to go.

"I didn't leave because you were too needy," she said. "Rhone? Stephen? I didn't find you too needy or anything of the sort. I left because I was starting to fall apart, and I worried that if I stayed, I would somehow infect you."

I turned back toward her, a woman sitting on the end of a wooden plank extending out into an endless ocean, corpses drifting lazily beneath her toes.

Then I stepped back up to her, leaned down, and . . . she kissed me. That old, familiar brush of the lips, followed by passion with her hand on my neck, pulling my face to hers. I let the emotion I'd guarded return, flood through me, the passion and even the pain. I pressed my lips to hers, let my skin touch hers, let my soul—briefly—touch hers.

I still loved her. That was real too.

She finally broke the kiss, pulling her head back an inch, staring into my eyes.

"You taught me," I said, "that I need to have purpose in life. I tried solving cases, but a part of me knew all along they wouldn't be enough." I took her hand. "But now, in this moment, I have a real purpose. A goal."

"What?"

"I'm going to find a way, Sandra. And when I do, I promise you, I'll come back. I'll do for you what you did for me. I'll bring you answers."

She shook her head. "Rhone . . ."

I squeezed her hand, then stood up and left her, taking the long walk back along the pier. It was so *strange* not to have a cluster of aspects around me, but I felt—already—the voices starting. The familiarity of the tones was fading away, becoming hisses and terrors.

I pushed back into the warehouse, feeling a dawning frustration and panic build inside me. How could I think to help her? I couldn't help myself.

I closed the door. Whispers hissed at me. For now I ignored them, returning to the fallen bodies of Kyle and his employees. I secured their guns—unloaded them and left them in one of the desk drawers—then I turned off the hallucination device.

Kyle immediately sat up, holding his side—poking it tenderly. He shot me a glare.

"You're going to leave me alone," I told him. "Don't contact me. Don't watch me." I walked toward the door. "But I intend to return, to visit a friend. When I do, you can study my brain—but only for the time I'm in the chamber with her. If you try to trap me again, there *will be consequences.*"

Kyle nodded. "I'm glad you've seen the advantages offered by our revolutionary new—"

"Oh, shut up." I stepped out into the night, hands in my pockets, feeling wrung out. Most of me had died tonight. And I had no idea what to do with the parts that were left.

I was alone. Actually *alone.*

I found that I didn't care for it. I walked down to the shadowy parking lot, then hesitated as I saw something moving nearby, hiding behind a bush. It looked like . . . a person.

"Jenny?" I said, shocked.

The aspect vanished the moment I saw her.

I sighed, but was a little surprised that one was actually left. I stood there until—unexpectedly—my limo pulled up beside me. Barb rolled down the window, and looked out. "We done here, sir?"

"I told you to leave."

"Uncle Wilson warned me that you might occasionally be . . . difficult. I figured I couldn't exactly *abandon* you, even if you were annoying." She held up a thermos. "Lemonade?"

"I . . ." I wrapped my arms around myself. "Thank you."

She hopped out and opened the door for me, but the back of

the limo looked cavernous without the aspects. Intimidating and cold.

"Could I sit up front?" I asked.

"Oh!" She opened the front passenger door. "Sure, I guess. But what about all the—"

"Don't worry about them," I said, settling into the seat. "Drive me . . . drive me to the corner of Fifty-Third and Adams."

"Isn't that where—"

"Yes."

I took the lemonade cup she poured, and it did taste a lot like Wilson's. She pulled the limo out onto the street, and we drove through a dark city; it was past eleven, approaching midnight. But it wasn't long before we pulled up beside the old building where I'd first met "Jenny" the reporter. I now saw it for what it was. An old abandoned building that might once have been an office structure.

"Park right there," I said, pointing to the curb. "A little farther forward . . ."

I climbed out and into the back of the hollow car, fishing in a bag on the floor. I finally came out with the camera. *Let's see . . . what time was it. . . .*

It took some fine-tuning to get it right. Barb had to pull the car forward a little, and I had to get the camera's timing dial just right. But eventually I snapped a photo, and it developed into a shot inside this very car from earlier in the day.

It showed me, Tobias, J.C., and Ivy. Laughing at something dumb J.C. had said, Ivy holding to his arm, Tobias grinning. I felt tears in the corners of my eyes.

Barb peeked in, looking over my shoulder.

"What do you see?" I asked.

"You, by yourself."

"I can still imagine them, in the right circumstances," I said, resting my fingers on the picture. "They're in my brain somewhere. How do I reach them?"

"You're asking me?" she asked. Then she perked up. "Oh! I totally forgot. Here, this is for you. He said to give it to you when you finished tonight." She reached into her pocket and took out a small envelope.

Inside was a small invitation to Wilson's birthday/retirement party. At the bottom, it said, "Admits fifty-two." With a smiley face.

"He said there's no obligation," she said. "But he wanted you to know you were welcome."

I touched the tears on my cheeks, then checked the time. "Eleven forty-five? Will it even still be going?"

"I'll bet it is," she said. "You know Wilson and his fondness for nightcaps. He'll be sitting with the family around the hearth, telling stories." She eyed me. "Only a few are about you."

You know Wilson. Did I? He'd just always been there, with lemonade.

"I can't go," I said. "I just . . ."

The objection died on my lips. She must have sensed that I didn't mean it, because she went to the front, then drove to Wilson's house. He had spent many nights at my mansion, sleeping there, but did have his own home. Or at least a room in his brother's house where he stayed sometimes. I wasn't sure who actually owned the place.

Barb pulled us into the driveway—the limo barely fit—and then led me in through the garage of the modest home. She entered, and true to her word I heard laughter inside. Saw the warm light of a fireplace burning, with people sitting around and chatting, drinking cider and lemonade—which was apparently a thing for them too.

I lingered on the threshold as Barb got some cake from the kitchen table, then tossed her coachman's cap onto the counter and went over to the fireplace. She leaned down beside a chair there, and soon a familiar lanky figure unfolded itself from the seat.

Wilson seemed genuinely happy to see me. He rushed over. "Sir? Sir, please, come in! You remember Doris and Stanley? And little Bailey—well, not so little anymore, but we still say that. And . . ."

"I'm sorry," I said, turning to go. "I shouldn't be here, interrupting time with family."

"Sir," Wilson said, catching my arm. "Stephen? But you *are* family."

"I . . ."

"Don't worry about the others!" he said, gesturing toward what— he imagined—must have been my aspects. "We have plenty of seats! Just let me know how many. Please, you've been so good to me over the years. It would be a *pleasure* to host you."

"I'm alone tonight," I whispered, feeling at my jacket pocket where I'd put the photo. "Just me."

"Alone?" Wilson asked. "Sir, what happened?"

"Can we talk about it another time? I think . . . I think I might just want to have some cake."

Wilson smiled, and soon I was sitting by the fire with his siblings, nieces, and nephew. Listening to him tell *his* version of the teleporting cat case, which was admittedly one of the better ones. I didn't eat much cake, but I did enjoy the warmth, the laughter, and—well—the *reality* of it all.

All the things that matter in life are the things that you can't measure. . . .

I found that I'd inadvertently lied to Wilson, because I wasn't alone. I caught Jenny hovering in the kitchen, both my newest aspect and my last. She had her notepad out again, and was furiously writing.

EPILOGUE

I didn't go back to the mansion that night.

I couldn't go there and face that void. That . . . or worse. Madness, shadows coming to life to torment me. I just . . . I wanted a few more hours to recover.

Fortunately, Wilson's family had a guest room, which they let me have for the night. I retired there once the stories ended, and turned on the room's desktop computer. I did a little research, skimming pages on Wikipedia on basic topics I'd once known. To see if there was anything left in my brain.

I found the holes erratic. Most of it seemed to be gone, but then I'd touch on something online, and before I knew it my fingers would be typing out a string of words. When I sat back to study them, I couldn't find the information in my brain—but I'd obviously typed it, so I had it somehow.

That was how it had been for me when I was younger, before

Sandra, and before the aspects. My brain tucked all of this knowledge away, but didn't know how to use it.

I slumped in the seat, overwhelmed and used up, frustrated and angry. "Is she right?" I said to the small, empty bedroom. "I promised to find a solution, but what hope do I have? Sandra knows way more than I do about this, and she couldn't find a solution."

No responses.

I took the photo from my pocket and propped it up on the computer keyboard. "Is this really it? I've lost them forever? Ivy, J.C., Tobias? Gone because my brain just doesn't feel up to the effort?"

"Not gone," Jenny said.

I spun my chair and found her standing in the shadows by the door. She held up her notepad. "I've got them right here."

"How are you still alive?" I said.

"You told me to go," she said. "You told me to go away, to break the rules. So I did. You preserved me."

"You're not a real aspect," I said. "I didn't summon you."

"Of course you did. The question is why." She stepped toward me, holding out the notepad. "What is it you wanted me to do? What's my expertise, Stephen Leeds?"

I looked away from the notepad. "I'll just end up repeating the cycle. It's either that or madness."

"False dichotomy," she whispered.

Pretending there were only two options, when there might be a third. Or more. I looked at the notepad, filled with scrawled notes. At the top of the page it read, *Tobias*.

She hadn't been taking notes on me, but on the aspects.

A *third way out*. A way to internalize the aspects, yet let them still live on? A way to be at peace with the voices, to give them an outlet other than to scream at me, ignored?

"I am an expert," Jenny said softly, "in them. In *you*. The sum expertise of a decade of living with them, and with this incredible, insane brain of yours." She proffered the notepad again. "Let them live again."

I took it, hesitantly. "It won't be the same."

"Make it the same."

"It won't be real."

"Make it real."

She faded. Leaving the notepad in my hand, filled with notes. Stories, lives. I didn't feel the sensation of ripping loss. The information was still there in my head. Her knowledge. My knowledge.

I looked at the glowing computer monitor. *This won't work*, I thought. *This can't work.*

. . . *Can it?*

I sat with the notepad under my hand, but I didn't need it. I just needed to know it was there. So I started typing.

My name is Stephen Leeds, I wrote, *and I am perfectly sane. My hallucinations, however, are all quite mad.*

I wrote for hours. Word after word after word. Somewhere near dawn, I saw a shadow reflected in the computer screen. When I turned, nobody was there, but when I looked back at the screen it was like I could see him behind me. I almost—but not quite—felt a hand rest on my shoulder. I didn't look away from the computer, but reached up, and touched the hand with mine. The hand of a man weathered with age.

Well done, Stephen, a familiar voice—not completely real—said in my mind. *Well done! Why don't you write about Ivy and J.C. going to Paris together? She's always wanted to go. Something will go wrong, of course. A diamond heist perhaps? The Regent Diamond is there, on display at the Louvre. It's said to be the clearest diamond in all the world. . . .*

I smiled. Sandra *was* wrong. It wasn't about containing them. It was about letting them free.

I hurriedly continued typing. My adventures are done. Finally, thankfully.

But my hallucinations . . . well, they're *always* getting into trouble.